Surprise!
The Continuing Adventures of a Young Cowboy

Stu Campbell

ISBN: 978-0-9675164-1-7

Edited by Mira Perrizo
Cover and text design by D.K. Luraas
Cover painting by Larry Jones, Bouse, Arizona
Author photo by Elizabeth Dobbs

Printed in the United States of America

Contents

Back Home

I was actually a little excited about school this year. I was scheduled to graduate in the spring and that was something to get excited about. I hadn't given much thought to what I was going to do after graduation, but I would be relieved to be out of school. And I did have a job for next year, at least for the summer, maybe longer.

I rode into our ranch and was at ease with the familiar surroundings. It was good to be home. I turned my burro and saddle horse loose in the horse pasture, put my saddle and pack saddle in the tack room and carried my stuff to the house. As I walked onto the porch, a voice rang out, "Is that you, Honey?" It was my mother.

Without thinking, I answered, "Yes."

I had been given the nickname "Honey" earlier in the summer by my girlfriend, and it had stuck. I still bristled at the term, but had become used to it and answered to it.

"You're the wrong Honey," she said, as she came out of the kitchen and gave me a hug. "But it's good to have you home. I was actually looking for your father. He said he'd be back about this time. Don't be tracking all those dirty clothes through the house. How are Sally and Bud?"

Sally is my girlfriend and Bud is her father. I had worked for them all summer. "They're fine," I said.

"You're home a little earlier than we figured," said Mother.

"I need to go to town and get some school supplies," I replied. I didn't want to tell my mother I really wanted to go to town and get Sally a hackamore for her Christmas present.

"You father's in town today. You should have written him and told him what you wanted, he could have picked it up for you." Sometimes mothers offer more help than what's actually needed.

"I probably ought to go myself," I said.

"I'm going in Tuesday. I can meet you after school and bring you home if you want. Are you doing your Christmas shopping early again this year?"

Mother was referring to the fact that last year I had bought, by mistake, a ladies shirt for myself to wear to school. When she brought the fact that it was a ladies shirt to my attention, I put the shirt in the top of the closet and forgot all about it until I received a Christmas present from Sally. I sent her the shirt, but Mother refused to believe that purchase was actually a mistake.

Unconsciously, I answered, "Yes." Both my mother and dad had met Sally last summer, so there was no need to keep her a secret as I had tried to in the past.

"What are you planning on getting her, another blouse?"

"No," I answered. "I'll get her something more practical. I was thinkin' a hackamore with a soft cotton mecate."

"But that was a mighty pretty blouse you got her last year."

I couldn't tell if my mother was joking with me or being serious.

"I know you still don't believe it, but that shirt was actually a mistake," I said.

"But it made a big hit with Sally! I sure do like her."

"Well, Mom, I sure do too," I said. "I guess I was just lucky when I bought the shirt. I really had intentions of returning it. Anything that needs doin' around here?"

I was beginning to feel a little uncomfortable with this conversation. I still wasn't used to talking about my girlfriend with anyone.

"No," said Mother, "you just relax and tell me about your summer. You didn't write as often as you said you would."

Actually, I didn't write at all. I was too busy with all my spare time being taken up with Sally.

"You saw what I did when you visited last summer. That was pretty much it."

It occurred to me that I hadn't told Mother about Sally and her horse being upended by a bull, so I related that incident to her. She was concerned, but pleased to find out Sally was all right.

Presently, Dad returned from town. "How was your summer, son?"

"You pretty well saw it when you were there," I said.

"He told me Sally and her horse were upended by a bull," said Mom. "According to him everything turned out all right. The Wilson ranch will have plenty of hamburger this winter."

Dad gave a knowing smile. "I'll bet," he said.

Turning to me, he asked, "Are you all set for school this year?"

"I do need some things from town," I answered.

"He's doing his Christmas shopping early again this year," chided my mother.

"Oh really! Do you need another shirt?"

I could see the grin on Dad's face and thought I would be in for some tough kidding. Before I could answer he continued, "Your mother is going in Tuesday, you can pick up what you need and ride home with her after school."

"That's what Mom said," I replied. It was uncanny the way my mother and dad thought along the same lines without seemingly discussing the subject previously. "I guess that will have to work. What's goin' on here? What do we have to do this weekend before school starts?"

"Just the regular ranch chores," said Dad. "It might be kinda boring for you after all the excitement of the dude ranch, all the people, a girlfriend, and a wild bull. This will be kinda tame."

School started and on Tuesday I made arrangements to meet Mom at the saddle shop after school. I went to the bank, deposited the check Bud had given me but kept the cash. I wasn't sure just how much a good hackamore would cost and I needed a headstall and a mecate. This was a special gift and it needed to be of high quality.

I always liked the saddle shop. There were lots of new saddles, bridles, and other horse gear and the smell of the new leather was always inviting. I didn't spend much time looking at the saddles, but went right to the bridle section where I could find the hackamores.

There was a good selection of bosals and I picked one that was a little heavier as I knew that the grulla Sally was riding had a stubborn streak in him. I passed on a lighter bosal that had some colored rawhide braided into it. I thought Sally might like the fancier one, but I also knew how practical she was.

I picked out a good headstall, and then Clarence, the owner of the saddle shop, offered to give me some help.

"Why don't you pick one of those hackamores that's already made up?"

"I'm makin' up one that's special," I said.

"Well," answered Clarence, "let me make up one for you that's made right, with a fiador and a mecate. That headstall you got will work, but not really good."

"It's a nice headstall," I said. "Sally will like it." I'd let it slip that I had a girlfriend and I hadn't intended to. I was becoming more comfortable with having a girlfriend.

"Are you making this up for a girl?" There was a big grin on Clarence's face. "Is she a special girl?"

"Sorta," I said. I toyed with the idea of trying to tell Clarence that Sally was a horse, but decided against it. Mother would be showing up soon and she would be sure to let the cat out of the bag, probably inadvertently, but still, the news would be out.

"Then you need a special bosal," said Clarence. "You just wait here, I'll be right back."

Clarence went to the back room. Our family had known Clarence for years and had done business in his saddle shop for as long as I could remember. He had made some major repairs to my dad's saddle when it had got tore up in a wreck.

Presently Clarence returned holding a new bosal with some colored strands of rawhide braided into it, complete with a fiador and a black and white soft cotton mecate.

"This is pretty enough to set any young horsewoman on her heels," he said as he handed me the hackamore. "You'll have any young lady chasing you all over the hills after this hackamore. And the mecate is soft cotton, not braided horsehair. That will keep her hands soft and she won't be scratching you when she runs her hands through the hair on your head. You still got hair on your head, don't you?"

Clarence did have a way with words when he was selling something.

Without thinking, I said, "I'll take it." Then, I added, "How much is it?"

"How much you got?"

I could see that Clarence was willing to dicker and assumed he probably had the outfit priced pretty high.

"I ain't got much, but it's a real nice outfit. I probably ought to stay with this other stuff. I think I can afford it."

"I'll make you a real good deal on this one and you'll have all the girls after you!" Clarence was wanting to sell this hackamore pretty bad. I began to wonder why. I looked at the price tag, and I could see why!

"I really can't afford this," I said.

"Don't look at that," said Clarence, ripping off the price tag. "I told you I'd make you a good deal!"

I asked, "What's a good deal?"

"I'll sell you this one for half price."

I took the hackamore and began to look it over closely. "What's wrong with it?"

"Nothing! You know I don't sell junk! Just ask your dad!"

"Okay, I'll take it," I said, hoping I had enough cash. "But I'll need a box for it."

"That's handled easily enough," said Clarence. "You want it gift wrapped, too?"

"No," I said. I didn't think he had any Christmas wrapping paper handy.

I spent the rest of the afternoon looking around the saddle shop while waiting for my mother. I saw a lot of stuff I would have liked, but I already had most of it, and although a lot of my equipment might have been old, it was still serviceable.

When Mother finally showed up, we left for the ranch.

"What did you get at the saddle shop?"

"I got a new hackamore," I answered.

"Did you break yours?"

"No," I answered. "It's for Sally." I had let it slip again and didn't intend to.

"A hackamore for Sally! Do you think she'll like it?"

"I'm sure she will. Clarence assured me any horsewoman would love it. Besides that, she doesn't have one and can use it on her grulla colt she's breaking."

After showing her the hackamore, Mother said, "But it's not as pretty as that blouse you bought her! I didn't realize you had such exquisite tastes!"

I was sure mother was trying to tease me, but I wasn't going to let her get away with it. Trying to change the subject, I said, "That reminds me, Bud and Pat are coming in October to pick out some replacement heifers an' Bud's bringin' his brother, Rod. We'll have to wean our calves a little early this year as we generally do that around Thanksgiving."

"That will be nice," said Mother. "Is Sally coming with them?"

My mother enjoyed talking about my girlfriend with me and I think she knew it made me a little uncomfortable. I think that's why she enjoyed talking about Sally so much. But every chance she got, she would bring up the subject of Sally. I certainly wasn't ashamed of Sally, I was almost constantly thinking of her myself. But when Mother brought up the subject, there was little else to think of.

We got back to the ranch and I resumed my normal ranch chores, before and after school.

One day, I reminded Dad that Bud was coming in October and he informed me of the date Bud would arrive. He was already on top of things.

"We might have to keep you out of school for a few days so we can get the cattle gathered, sort and wean the calves and get them used to eating out of a feed bunk. Do you think you could miss some school without missing some education? We might have to keep Tommy out also."

"I could do that all right! It will be a pleasure!"

My dad replied, "Will you still graduate with honors?"

"I don't know about honors," I said, "but I'll be honored to just graduate! It seems like I've been goin' to school all my life."

"You almost have," said Dad. "Have you given any thought to what you're going to do after graduation, if you do graduate?"

Dad was teasing me, I was going to graduate. However, he was aware of how difficult some of my studies had been for me.

"Yes, I'll graduate. I haven't really thought about what I'd do after graduation. Bud wants me to come back to work for him next summer, he'll have a few more colts to start an' plenty of dudes. I don't know what'll happen after that. I hadn't thought about it much, I've been so busy studyin'."

I was trying to give some fun back to my dad. He knew what kind of a student I was.

"You just let me know what days you want me an' I'll be glad to skip school for you," I said.

I could see my dad grinning at my comment and I had to laugh a little myself. If I could make my dad believe I was doing him a favor, I might be able to skip more school.

Sally's letters arrived on a regular basis, generally on Monday and I would answer them on Tuesday, during study period. She really didn't have anything to say other than how her school was going and what her friends were doing. She did say that she had ridden her grulla quite a bit before she left for school.

The middle of October arrived and I got out of school for a few days to help gather cattle. Although it was a little cold, it was nice to be horseback and out of school. Gathering the cattle wasn't hard; a lot of them were ready to come home as the nights were getting cold.

Two days after we had the cattle gathered, and sorted off the heifers from the cows, Bud, Pat, and Rod showed up. We'd turned the cows and the steer calves, along with some smaller heifer calves we knew Bud wouldn't want, out on the hayfields. "It's a little early, but we'll keep them here until we wean the other calves. It'll be easier than gathering them again in a month or so. There's plenty of feed," said Dad.

Bud was still using his cane from when he'd broken his foot earlier in the spring. Pat had done the driving. Bud had some boxes he gave to Tommy and me with the comment, "Put these in your freezer."

Tommy asked, "What are they?"

"That's hamburger," replied Bud. "That's from the bull that took Sally last summer. I can't wait to get rid of him."

"How is Sally?" I was anxious to find out about my girlfriend, but didn't want to appear too anxious.

"She's in school," answered Bud. "She did tell me to tell you 'Hello.' She also gave me this note to give you."

Bud handed me an envelope, and I immediately recognized Sally's handwriting. I put the envelope in my pocket.

"Aren't you going to read it? I'm sure you're interested in what she has to say," said Bud.

"I'll read it later," I said. "I've got to put this meat in the freezer before it thaws." I wasn't really in a rush to put the meat away, but I didn't want to read Sally's letter in front of a crowd. I guess I was still a little bashful.

We had a good time at supper that night. My dad had to relate how he had shot a mountain lion the winter before. Rod, Bud's brother, had lost some of his sheep to a mountain lion and he had run off a lion that was attacking my burro and her colt when I was on the trail. We had all assumed it was the same one and I proudly showed off the tanned hide and head hanging in the hallway. I had heard the story before, but Dad was adding a few details I hadn't heard. I really think he was embellishing the story a little for Rod's sake. I hadn't realized what a storyteller he was.

When I asked him about it later, he didn't readily admit to exaggerating the story, but he did say, "A good cowboy never lets the truth stand in the way of a good story!" He had a grin on his face when he said this, and I knew he was telling the truth, but in a humorous manner.

Bud was going to select some replacement heifers from our calf crop. That's why we were gathering early. Bud had bought some heifers for replacements some years earlier and Bud had liked them.

It wasn't until after supper that I had a chance to read Sally's letter. It started out,

Dearest Honey,

I thought, *At least that's better than My Dear Stupid, Dumb Loving Cowboy, like she had started out her letters last year.* Her letters this fall all started out with "Dearest Honey." I was getting used to the nickname.

> *I thought I would save a few cents and send this with Dad. I got a letter from Marie shortly after you left and she told me that Dave and her were planning on getting married when they graduated from school this fall. What do you think of that?*

Dave and Marie had worked for the Wilson's the previous summer and the fact that they became engaged didn't surprise me at all. I thought it might be a good idea.

The letter continued,

> *I think we'll be invited to the wedding. Do you want to go? I think it will be interesting to see you in a suit and tie. Send me a letter when Daddy gives you this so I can make plans.*
>
> *Make sure you talk to my dad about working next year. I know he wants you back and I do too! Do you want to get together at Christmas? It would be our first Christmas together. I think I'll be at the ranch this Christmas.*
>
> *Love,*
> *Sally*

I wondered why Sally had sent this with her dad rather than including it in one of her other letters. Perhaps Bud didn't know about Dave and Marie. I had no idea, but decided to keep my mouth shut and find out from Sally through the mail. The Christmas idea did sound good though.

The next morning we were up early and had the heifers in the corral. Tommy was sent to school and Bud, Pat, Rod, Dad, and I sorted the calves. Bud and Pat made the selections, Rod and Dad worked the gates, and I was given the job of hurrying the calves to the proper pen. Rod was working a gate into a pen where the calves would need a second look, Dad was working a gate to a pen that were definite purchase heifers. It was tiresome work, each heifer had to be looked at individually and her merits weighed between Bud and Pat. I made a lot of trips up and down that alley and decided that after lunch, I'd saddle Roman and make it easier on myself.

Bud and Pat selected about fifty heifers and decided that was enough. They decided against looking through the pen that needed a second look, they already had more than they needed. But they did take a second look through the "keepers" and cut their selection down to forty-five.

At lunch, I asked Bud why he was picking so many heifers.

"These girls are going to a feedlot," he said. "They'll be put on a special ration so they'll grow and then, if they weigh more than six hundred and fifty pounds in the spring, they'll be bred artificially as yearlings so they'll calve as two year olds."

"That's just invitin' calvin' problems, ain't it?" I was curious about this.

"I don't think so," said Bud. "There's been some research done in this field and it looks pretty promising. One big factor is getting the heifers to the proper weight then breeding them to a bull that's known to throw smaller calves. The research is pretty positive and Pat has talked with some folks that did it a year ago."

"Yeah," said Pat. "They said there were some calving problems, but by and large it worked good for them. And they expect to get an extra calf out of every cow over the course of the cow's life. That makes a big difference when you realize most range cows are culled by the time they're ten years old or earlier."

"I see," I said. I could see that my dad was listening pretty close to this conversation. My dad was really interested and asked, "What about the heifers rebreeding after they've calved as two year olds?"

"These heifers will be bred to calve thirty to forty-five days before the regular cow herd," interjected Bud. "That will give them extra time to recover and put on some weight before breeding season. Then they can calve right along with the older cows."

"But it's hard to put weight on a cow that's making milk and raising a calf," said Dad.

"Well," said Bud, "we have to raise the nutrition level on these heifers so they can rebreed as three year olds."

I could see that my dad was giving this subject some serious thought. I imagined the thought of an extra calf over the life of a cow appealed to him.

"There'll be a truck here in the morning to take the heifers to the feedlot. We won't have anything to do with them until after they're bred and come to the ranch along in June. If you're interested, I could send you the information I received about this. It is interesting and it breaks everything down into simple terms, even costs."

"I'd like that," said my dad.

There was a little snow starting to fall as we went to the house for the noon meal.

"If you don't mind," said Bud, "we'll stay tonight and help get the heifers loaded then leave when the calves leave. There's supposed to be a truck here around ten in the morning."

"That's fine," said Dad, as we entered the house. "You can stay as long as you want. You've brought your own beef, although I think my wife was planning on feeding you better than feeding you your own hamburger."

"You bet I was," said mother. "I've got a special surprise for lunch and an even more special surprise for supper."

"That's good," said Bud. "I'm getting tired of eating on that old bull and can't wait until he's all gone!"

Something to be Thankful For

The next morning we were all up early, waiting for the cattle trucks to show up. The conversation was mostly about getting an extra calf out of a cow over her lifetime. I found it very interesting and could see how it would add to the profitability of a cow-calf operation. I didn't have much to say about the idea, but was learning a lot just listening.

Presently, Pat said, "Come over here, Honey. I need to talk to you."

I thought he wanted to talk about the colts I had started for them last year, so I said, "One of them colts buck you off?"

"Don't be silly," answered Pat. "None of them colts could buck off a wet saddle blanket! But what I wanted to talk to you about was Sally."

I immediately thought something was wrong, maybe she found a new boyfriend or something.

"Is she okay?" I was trying to act like nothing was wrong, preparing myself for the worst.

"She's fine," replied Pat. "But she did want me to mention something to you about, ah … let's see, ah … just what was it?"

I thought, even though I knew he was having his fun with me, *Hurry up Pat. What was it?*

"Let's see, I might have forgotten it," continued Pat. "I think it had something to do with the holidays, I think, maybe Christmas. Yeah, that's it, Christmas. What you goin' to get me for Christmas?"

I blurted out, "What did Sally have to say?" I almost yelled, I was so anxious to hear what she had said and I said it so loud that my dad, Bud, and Rod overheard and started walking toward Pat and me.

I could see Pat was enjoying this little episode and he wasn't going to let me out of this embarrassment easily. "Oh! She wanted me to find out what your plans are for Christmas."

"Christmas! It ain't even Thanksgivin' yet! Why?"

"I think she said something about coming out for Christmas," said Pat.

"Why sure, she can come out here for Christmas," I said.

"No, no," said Pat. "I think she wants you to come to our place for the holidays."

Sally had mentioned getting together for Christmas, and I was not surprised Pat knew about it. Bud and Rod probably also knew.

"I hadn't given the holidays any thought," I said. This wasn't exactly true; I'd bought Sally her Christmas gift in September. "I don't know what my folks have planned, an' there's plenty to do around here."

"You better get it all done so you can come for the holidays," said Bud. "Sally's counting on it and it might be nice to have some extra help around although there won't be much to do. Pat will be busy halter breaking the weaner colts and they'll be some cow feeding to do. It will be just like a vacation for you."

"I'll have to see what my folks have to say about it," I said, looking at my dad.

"I'll have to see what your mother has to say about it," said Dad.

"You be nice to your mom and maybe she'll let you come," said Bud.

15

"I'm always nice to her," I said.

"Well, I understand you had to do the dishes last winter so she'd teach you how to dance," said Bud. "You might want to help her that way again. It might help your chances."

I could tell my mother and Sally had discussed me quite thoroughly the previous summer. I knew that they were talking about something on their rides together, but I only suspected until now that it was me. Now I knew. And I could tell Bud was quite knowledgeable about women.

"I don't know how I'd get there," I said. "It'll be too cold to ride Roman an' it'll take too long."

"I bet we can handle that, if you can come," said Bud.

I noticed my dad nodding in silent agreement, with a slight grin on his face.

The cattle trucks arrived. We loaded the heifers and Bud, Pat, and Rod made ready to leave.

Rod did tell me that the colts he borrowed from Bud worked real well for him last summer. "I tried to buy 'em, but Bud said they were goin' to make too good of dude horses. He wanted too much money for 'em. You did too good a job breakin' them for him."

I was glad to hear that, I was actually quite proud of my horse training skills.

"What should I tell Sally about the holidays? It's all right with me if you come," said Bud.

"Tell her that if she comes here for Thanksgiving, I'll do my darnedest to be there for Christmas!" I was surprised at my answer. I didn't even have permission to have overnight guests, but was extending an invitation. And to a young lady!

"I'll bet that will work," said Bud. "We'll be in touch, although I know you hear from Sally more frequently than I do!"

Bud, Pat, and Rod left. It was about a five-hour drive to the

Wilson ranch. I figured they'd get there about three-thirty or four o'clock.

"We'd better go have a talk with your mother," said Dad. "This might cause her some consternation and it's certainly going to be new to her. I don't know that she's going to go for this idea over Thanksgiving or Christmas."

"That's good," I said. "It's too late to try an' go to school now. Maybe you can help me talk Mother into this deal?"

"You're on your own there, son. You figure out what to say and how to say it." There was a little grin on my dad's face as he said this.

I was a little apprehensive about approaching Mother on the subject. The Christmas season was her favorite holiday and she really looked forward to it. I didn't know how she would react to my wanting to be gone during her favorite holiday.

I thought I'd try an approach on Mother that might make it sound like I was needed at the Wilson ranch over the holidays. "Bud an' Pat asked me if I could get away during the holidays to give them a hand with the weaner colts. Do you think I should go?"

"I don't know, son. There's a lot to do here and the holidays are special—a family time." Mother had a slight grin on her face as she said this. "Do you want to be away from your family at this time?"

"I think it's fairly important to Bud that I'm there."

Mother asked, "How come it's important to him?"

"I don't know," I said. "Maybe he's plannin' on breakin' a leg or somethin'."

Mother laughed. "I don't think that's the plan. But I do know what the plan is. I talked to Sally on the phone a while ago and she asked about your going to the Wilson's for Christmas."

"Oh really! I suppose I would have to be gift wrapped!"

I could see that Mother and Sally already had this planned out and my mom was having some fun with me. "What did you tell her?"

"That might be interesting to see you gift wrapped," said Mother. "I told her that I'd have to talk to your father and you about it. I wasn't sure just how either one of you would react to the situation. And, I wasn't sure just how you would get there."

I surmised that Mother was having a little fun with Sally also.

"Bud said he could get me there, if I could come," I said. "I think I'd like to go, I could be a big help to 'em."

Mother laughed again. "I'm sure that's the primary reason you want to go!"

I was in a spot. I didn't know what to say. I really didn't want to tell Mother that I'd rather spend the holidays with Sally than with my own family but that was the truth.

Then, I blurted out, "I told Pat and Bud that if Sally could come out here for Thanksgiving, I'd be there for Christmas." I didn't know what to expect when I said this. I felt like I had just dropped a bomb.

I was surprised when Mother said, "Why I think that's a wonderful idea! I'm surprised I didn't think of it when I talked to Sally on the phone."

"When did you talk to her?"

"She called a few days ago, before you got home from school," said Mother. "That's a great idea. I've already talked to your father about it and he thinks he and Tommy could handle the chores while you're gone. They seem to have been getting along fairly well while you've been gone during the summer. Tommy has been accepting more responsibility in your absence."

Mother's last comment stung just a little. I thought I was almost indispensable to this ranch. But, I passed this thought off with thoughts of spending the holidays with Sally.

"I'd better call her and see what she thinks of this new plan," said Mother.

I asked, "New plan?"

"Oh yes," replied Mother. "We already made plans for the holidays. Thanksgiving will be a new plan."

"You mean I can go?"

"Only if you want to," answered Mother. "But your plan about Sally being here for Thanksgiving might sour the deal. What if she can't come? You told Bud that you'd be there if Sally could come here."

"I can be there regardless," I said. "I'll start planning on how to get there."

"Take that up with your father," said Mother. "He might have some thoughts on it." Mother had a little grin on her face when she said that and I guessed that they had already discussed the situation and had arrived at a solution.

"Perhaps I should call Sally an' set up the deal," I said.

"No, I'll call her tomorrow or the next day while you're in school. She's in a different time zone you know. I'll let you know when I talk to her."

I decided I had enough time to write Sally a letter before I needed to start doing chores. It was hard to write, I was kind of excited. But I did write her and chastised her for being so secretive about the situation. I asked her in the letter just how long she and my mother had been planning things behind my back. I told her it was unfair to be planning things about me without consulting me. And I did tell her I was coming for Christmas. I also asked her if Bud knew about Dave and Marie planning on getting married. The letter turned out to be fairly long, longer than any of my other compositions to her. I wondered what she would think when she saw a fat letter arrive from me.

Tommy got home from school and we started the evening chores. The next few days were the same routine—school and chores. I anxiously awaited Sally's answer to my fat letter, tried to figure out how I would get to the Wilson ranch during the holidays, and waited for my mother to tell me she had talked to Sally. The Wilson ranch was about a five-hour drive from our ranch, longer if the weather was bad. I was kinda perplexed with this problem.

Sally's letter arrived and she claimed innocence with regard to planning behind my back with my mother, although she did own up to originating the idea of me going there for Christmas. She was in favor of the Thanksgiving idea, she thanked me for it, but she would have to talk to her dad. She called him once a week and she would let me know. She also told me Bud knew about Dave and Marie.

In her next letter, which came a week later, she accused me of plotting behind her back with her father about her coming to our place for Thanksgiving. Her father knew all about the plan that she would come out for that holiday. I hadn't been plotting with Bud about her coming out for Thanksgiving, the idea just popped into my head while Pat, Bud, and I were discussing going to the Wilson ranch for Christmas. I knew this was true, but found it difficult to explain on paper.

About a week before Thanksgiving, my dad said, "I want you to come to town with me on Saturday. Think you can handle it?"

"Yep," I said, "but Friday might be easier. I'll already be in town an' you can just get me out of school early." I was always looking for a legitimate excuse to get out of school.

"No," said Dad. "This job I've got in mind might take most of the day."

"I could stay out of school all day, if you need me," I said.

"Nope," said Dad. "This is a weekend job."

"What is it?"

"You'll find out Saturday."

There had been a lot of mysterious doings going on lately

around our ranch, a lot of grins between my mom and dad and I wasn't really aware of what was happening. I was busy with school, homework, ranch chores, and trying to solve the problem of getting to the Wilson's during the winter.

When Saturday arrived, we got the chores done and, after an extra cup of coffee, Dad and I headed to town. I had no idea what the plan was and knew better than to pester my dad with questions. I would find out soon enough. When we arrived in town, our first stop was at a car dealership. My first thought was that Dad must be gettin' a new truck.

"Come with me," said Dad.

We walked around the new trucks, just looking. I'll have to admit, they did look good, but the sticker prices were a little shocking. *It would be nice to have one,* I thought, *but I'll bet it would take a lifetime to pay for it.*

"I'm afraid these new trucks are a little out of my budget for what I've got in mind," said Dad. "Let's see what they've got in used trucks."

We went to the used truck area and Dad started looking at each truck a little closer. Occasionally, he would ask me, "What do you think of this one?"

I had no idea what he was shopping for and questioned him a little about what he was looking for. He didn't say.

Finally, I said, "If you're lookin' for another ranch truck, why not get a flatbed? You can carry more on 'em an' it's easier to load, especially if you're loadin' hay. That's what I'd do."

"Good idea, son. How's this one look to you?" he was standing by an older model flatbed truck.

"I suppose it'll do," I said. I figured my job was going to be driving a vehicle back to the ranch.

A salesman showed up and Dad knew him. As a matter of fact, Dad knew just about everyone in town.

"We'd like to take this one for a test drive," said Dad.

The salesman said, "We've actually got a better flatbed out back. Just took it in on trade last week. We haven't got it cleaned up yet, but it's a better truck."

"Let's see it," said Dad.

We walked around back. The truck the salesman showed us was a better looking truck, it didn't have as many dings on the body as the first one we looked at and the paint was in better shape.

"The previous owner is supposed to bring in the side racks for it next week. There's also a spare tire for it," said the salesman.

"Let's take it for a test drive," said Dad, as he climbed in the cab. "Get in, son."

"I'll get the keys," said the salesman.

Presently, we were driving the truck around town. Dad was very quiet, listening to the engine transmission and such. Soon he said, "Why don't you drive her a little and tell me what you think? Let's take her out in the country and see what she's like."

I got behind the wheel and started driving, heading out of town. I'd got my driver's license last fall when I got back in school. I hadn't driven much on the country roads or in town, but I'd driven our vehicles all over the ranch for a few years. I was already familiar with gear patterns. As far as I could tell, the truck handled good.

"What do you think, son?"

"I guess it's all right," I replied.

"Do you like it?"

"I think it's all right, but I don't know if I'd use it to go to town in." I had no idea why Dad was questioning me about this truck, when he knew more about mechanics and such than I did.

"I didn't ask you if you'd use it to go to town. I asked you if you liked it."

"I guess," I said. "It does seem to run all right."

"Good," said Dad. "We'll see about buying it for you."

"For me!" I was totally shocked and couldn't believe it. "For me?"

"Yes, son," said Dad. "Your mother and I decided to get you a vehicle for Christmas, and because of the developments about Thanksgiving and Christmas, we decided to give it to you now. Of course, you won't get anything on Christmas, but that shouldn't matter, you'll be at the Wilson's then."

I looked the truck over more closely. It would need to be cleaned up, but it did look pretty nice. I wanted to make sure we got the spare tire for it and the racks. I wondered what the racks looked like.

We found the salesman and I listened as he and Dad haggled over the selling price. There wasn't much haggling as they knew each other and they also knew about how far the other one would go.

When Dad said, "But it's for my son, and I don't know if he's worth that much," the salesman dropped the price some more and the deal was made.

I was ready to drive the truck home, but the salesman objected. "We want to clean this up for you, seeing as this is your first vehicle. And we need to get the side racks put on. You come back next Saturday and your truck will be ready for you."

Dad agreed and the deal was made. "We'll bring in your mother, Tommy, and Betty and do a little early Christmas shopping," said Dad.

On the way home, Dad told me what the terms of my ownership of the new truck were going to be. They'd add me to their insurance policy, but I'd have to pay them the added cost.

"You'll also be responsible for the upkeep costs," said Dad. "That means you'll have to buy six tires rather than four because the truck is a one-ton dual-wheeled truck. It'll cost you a little more. You'll have to change the oil regularly and the oil filter. I'll show you how to do it. And you'll be responsible for everything else. Make sure you thank your mother for that gift," added Dad.

"I think I can do that," I said. "And I sure want to thank you, too!"

We got back to the ranch and I couldn't wait to tell Mother what a wonderful gift she had gotten me for Christmas. She seemed pleased.

"Oh, by the way, Sally called."

"What did she say?" I could hardly contain my excitement.

"She said she will be out here for Thanksgiving. She will be arriving the Wednesday before Thanksgiving about one o'clock. The way I have it planned, you can take your new truck to school that day, leave school at lunch and pick her up at the bus station. Then when you get her, you can return to school and continue your studies and introduce her to your friends. I'm sure they'd all love to meet her."

"What?! Return to school!" I had missed seeing the grin on my mother's face.

"No," said mother laughing. "You bring her directly home when you pick her up. I haven't seen her since last summer and am anxious to see her again. We have some visiting to catch up on."

Mother's last comment was a relief. I really didn't want to go to school when Sally was here.

I couldn't wait for the Wednesday before Thanksgiving to come. Not so much to get out of school early, but to spend some time with Sally.

A week after we bought the truck, the family went to town to pick it up and do some Christmas shopping. I was very surprised at the truck. The stock racks were on and they had been freshly painted red. The truck really looked nice and I was the owner!

"We had the racks painted, just for you," said the salesman. "Looks pretty good, doesn't it?"

When the much anticipated Wednesday arrived, I made sure I put on my newest clothes. I wanted to look my best for Sally! It seemed like my school classes dragged throughout the morning. When noon finally arrived, I didn't have anything to eat; I went straight to my truck then straight to the bus station. I knew I had about an hour to wait, but that was all right. I would take Sally to lunch. Our first dinner date!

Sally's bus finally arrived, just a little early, but to me it seemed late. As far as I was concerned, it wasn't early enough. Sally got off and came running to me.

"Honey," she yelled, "Honey!" I braced myself, thinking she might knock me down, but she slowed down, wrapped both arms around me and began smothering me with kisses.

Everyone at the bus station turned and looked. I could feel my face flushing; I was starting to blush.

By now I should have been used to these affectionate displays in public on Sally's part, but was still uncomfortable with them. Finally she stopped, took a step back and asked, "How are you? It's so good to see you!"

I caught my breath and said, "I'm fine. How are you?" I didn't have to ask, she looked good to me. She always did.

She grabbed me again and started kissing again. I wasn't suffering; I was kind of enjoying it, but I was embarrassed.

"Miss, miss." It was the bus driver, tapping Sally on the shoulder as he spoke. "Your bags are over here."

"Oh, thank you," said Sally. She gave the driver fifty cents and started toward the bags.

"I'll get them," I said. She had two bags and a handbag. I got the bags and was surprised at how heavy they were. *Perhaps she's plannin' on stayin' more than four days,* I thought. And I also thought that would be nice.

I took the bags and led Sally to my truck. I opened the passenger side door, helped her in, put the bags in the back and climbed into the cab. I was surprised that Sally had moved to the center of the seat, barely allowing me enough room to get in.

"I'll drive us home," I said.

"Don't you want me to sit next to you?"

"Oh yes," I said. "But I just need a little more room. I ain't all the way in yet. Have you eaten yet?"

Sally slid over, allowing me to get in the truck.

"No, I'm starved! They don't feed you much on the airplane and nothing on the bus. I didn't have time to get anything between the airport and the bus station."

"What do you want?"

"Anything!"

"How's something from the hamburger joint by school sound?" I hadn't given much thought as to where we could get something to eat. "They have stuff besides hamburgers, an' I can show you around this little town on the way."

"Sounds good to me," said Sally.

I drove straight to the hamburger joint by the school because we were both hungry and I pointed out the points of interest on the way. There really weren't many attractions in this little town.

Attempting to make conversation, I said, "I thought you'd be travelin' in a dress, but you got jeans on."

"Your mother told me you'd be picking me up and I didn't know you had a truck. I thought you'd come horseback and ..."

I interrupted, "Horseback! You know, we are civilized on this side of the mountain!"

"Yes," she said, "but you've always showed up at the ranch horseback. I thought you preferred that mode of transportation."

"Maybe you're right," I said. "Your bags are pretty heavy, how long are you planning on staying?"

"Four days. I do have to be back to school by Tuesday. As it is, I'll only miss two days, Wednesday and Monday."

As we got to the hamburger joint, I said, "You could stay longer if you wanted to."

Sally grinned, but didn't say anything.

The ride to the ranch was leisurely after eating. I took my time driving. Sally was right next to me and had her arm around me. I didn't see any need to rush home. Much to my surprise, Tommy was already home from school when we arrived at the ranch.

I carried Sally's bags into the house while Mother and Sally hugged and became reacquainted.

"I better go help Tommy an' Dad with the evening chores," I said.

"Let me get a heavier coat and I'll help," said Sally.

"That's not necessary," said Mother. "There's not that much to do, they can handle it, and we need to catch up on some visiting. You can help a little tomorrow if you want to."

Supper that night was spent with Sally, Mother, and Betty doing most of the talking. I really didn't have much to say, as I'd done a lot of talking with Sally on the drive home. After supper, Sally said, "Show me your ranch."

Sally and I walked outside, with Sally holding my hand.

"I don't want to get lost," she said.

"Don't be out late," said Mother. "It's cold out there and we can't have you getting sick."

We went to the barn and once inside, Sally immediately kissed me. I assumed we were going to resume our kissing practice that we had been doing every night at the Wilson ranch. And we did. She was the most kissing person I ever met. After a little more practice, we headed back to the house.

On the way back to the house, Sally asked me, "What's the plan for the holidays and how can I help?"

"Generally," I said, "we sorta take it easy on Thanksgiving then gather cattle and sort calves on Friday, Saturday, and Sunday. We don't have to do a lot of gatherin' this year as we gathered early so your dad could select some replacement heifers. All the cattle are on the hayfields. I imagine we'll corral the cattle, sort the calves and wean 'em. It shouldn't be too tough. We'll ship the calves in another week or two. If you want to help, you can ride my horse, Roman, an' help gather the hayfields."

"What will you ride?" Sally asked.

"I can ride anything on this ranch," I said. I wasn't really bragging, we had some extra horses and they were all gentle. "I don't think Dad will mind if I ride one of his horses."

"If that's the plan, I can help your mother fix the meal tomorrow," said Sally.

That's what I liked about Sally, she was always ready to help with anything. And she could do anything.

Thanksgiving day came. Dad, Tommy, and I did the ranch chores while Sally, Mother, and Betty started to prepare the main meal.

"You boys find something to do while we're working here and stay out of our way," said Mother as Dad, Tommy, and I entered the house.

"I believe it would be wise to park in the living room and watch the football game," said Dad. His tone indicated that Tommy and I should also go to the living room and stay out of the way.

Before mealtime, Sally had slipped away and changed her clothes. She put on a dress. I had only seen her in a dress once before and it had left a good impression. She was even prettier today than she was when I had first seen her in a dress. Even my dad was impressed. I had a hard time finding my mouth with a forkful of food for looking at Sally.

The next day, I saddled Roman for Sally. We had a few extra

saddles and I used one that I thought would be comfortable for her. When she got on, I adjusted her stirrups.

"You know," I said, "I do this all summer long for the dudes an' now I'm doin' it for a guest here an' we ain't even a dude ranch!"

Sally made a swing with her foot and almost kicked me, but she was smiling. "You're terrible," she said.

I saddled another horse for myself and we gathered the hayfields. I watched Sally and Roman closely. I knew Roman wouldn't give Sally any problems, but I really like to watch Sally ride. As we rode away from the barn, it started to snow lightly.

When the cattle were corralled, we separated the cows from the calves, turned the cows out into a hayfield farther away from the house, unsaddled the horses and called it a day until it was time to do the evening chores.

At supper, Dad said, "That's been the easiest gather and weaning that we've had. We really don't have anything real pressing to do. So, tomorrow, I want you two to ride the outside, the beginning of the summer range, and look for any cows or calves we may have missed. If you find anything, just bring it home and turn it in with the cows. Make sure you dress warm; it's supposed to be colder tomorrow. It should be fairly easy to see any tracks with the new snow on the ground."

I had thought we'd pretty well gathered everything. Dad hadn't said anything about missing any cattle, but I suppose it was a job that needed to be done.

The next day, Sally and I headed out to double check the summer range. I put on a Scotch cap and found one for Sally. Both of them had earmuffs. Along the way, we passed Matilda and Sassy.

"Are you going to bring Matilda to the ranch next summer?"

"If you folks want her, I can," I said.

"Oh yes," said Sally, "we want her. She made a lot of kids

and their parents happy last summer. She was perfect in her job as a 'leader.' And she's real gentle."

"I'll bring her, if she doesn't die this winter. You know, she's gettin' pretty old."

"If she dies, bring Sassy," said Sally.

"I can't do that," I said. "I gave Sassy to Betty last year for Christmas. She's not mine."

"Then you better take good care of Matilda!"

We rode the lower parts of the summer range looking for cow tracks in the snow. We didn't see any tracks or cows, but we did see a lot of deer. It was a nice ride and it didn't get too cold although the day stayed overcast all day. And we had a good talk.

It started with Sally asking, "What do you think about Dave and Marie getting married after school?" She looked and sounded very serious as she spoke.

"That sounds like an interesting after-school activity," I said.

"Don't be silly!"

Apparently Sally was being serious, but she did have a grin on her face.

"I guess it's all right," I said. "What are they goin' to do? Do they have jobs? Do they have a place to live? Have they given it much thought? That's a pretty serious move on their part. Are they ready for it?"

"I don't know the answer to all those questions," said Sally. "I just asked you what you thought of it."

"I guess it's all right," I said. Trying to be funny, I added, "I've heard it said that marriage is an institution an' those people that enter into it are instantly institutionalized."

I looked at Sally as I said this. She grinned, but still had a very serious look on her face.

"Do you want to go to the wedding? It's going to be in New Hampshire, at Marie's, in June."

"I don't think I'll be able to make it. I've never been to New

Hampshire an' don't think I really want to go. Besides, I think I've got a job, for the summer at least, an' I'd have to ask my boss."

Sally looked surprised. "Where are you working?"

"Actually," I said, "I'm workin' for your dad."

"Well," said Sally, "if you're working for my dad, then I'm your boss and I say you should go!"

"Hold on there, Darlin'! I'm …"

Sally interrupted, "Darling! Do you realize that's the first time you've called me Darling, Honey?"

I was starting to blush. "Well, it just ah … sorta, ah … slipped out."

"You mean you didn't intend to call me Darling, Honey?"

"I didn't really want to say it so as you'd hear it," I said.

"Do you mean to tell me you've been calling me names behind my back?"

"No," I said. I was blushing fairly hard now and felt like I was being put on the spot. "The names I call you when you're not around are very, very complimentary to you."

She asked, "Like what?"

"I can't really tell you, 'cause then you'd know. But there's nothing wrong with them." Trying to change the subject and not be subjected to more embarrassment, I said, "Lets move these horses out a little, we're not covering much ground an' we got a ways to go yet."

I spurred my horse into an easy lope and Sally, riding Roman, didn't have any trouble keeping up. After about a hundred yards or so, long enough for my blush to fade away, I slowed my horse back to a walk.

"That was fun," said Sally. "What are your plans after graduation? You are going to graduate, aren't you?"

It was my turn to laugh. "I'm figurin' on it, although I don't imagine I'll graduate with honors. But it will be an honor to graduate. I haven't made any plans after graduation, other than

31

to work for your dad. After that, I don't know. What are your plans?"

"My dad wants me to go to college and I guess I could. But I'm not really that interested in it. I'd like to be outside more and even though I did well in school, I'm not interested in higher education. I'd like to stay at the ranch year round and be involved with everything there. That's where my real interests lie."

I interjected, "You mean I'm not your real interest?"

Sally laughed. "After you, the ranch is my real interest. And Dad will need some extra help. His foot hasn't healed properly. He's thinking of going in and having it broken again so it can heal right." Sally again got a serious look on her face.

"He was still usin' the cane when he came to pick out his replacement heifers," I said.

Sally looked troubled and I wasn't used to seeing her this way. I didn't know what to say. "Lets move these horses out some more!" I thought a little more action might help her feel better.

We loped the horses another hundred yards then slowed to a walk.

"So," said Sally, "you won't go to the wedding with me?"

"I don't see as how I can. I will have some responsibility to your dad. However, I would if I could and could afford it."

That answer brought a smile to Sally's face and her mood seemed to brighten up considerably.

We continued riding, not seeing any signs of cattle, but having good conversation. Some how or another, the subject kept coming back to Dave and Marie and their wedding. I thought that their wedding was causing Sally some problem, but decided not to press the question.

We rode back to the ranch and turned our horses loose. I offered to unsaddle Roman for her, but she refused.

"I'll take care of my own horse," she said.

"But that's my horse and you're our guest! I need to be doin' that for you," I countered.

"But I'm not a dude!"

"Still, it's only proper that I do that for my girlfriend, ain't it, Darlin'?"

"It might be, Honey, but it's still my job," she said. "And that's the second time you've called me Darling!"

"No it ain't," I said.

"Oh? How many times have you called me that when I wasn't around?"

"I don't know," I said. "I lost track. I didn't know I was supposed to keep track of 'em." I was starting to blush again and wanted to change the subject before Sally noticed. But she saw.

"You're still my sweet bashful, awkward, shy cowboy, aren't you?"

"Ah ... well ... I guess so," I replied.

"Don't ever change," she said.

I was hoping I would change. I was uncomfortable blushing so easily and constantly feeling like I needed to change the subject when I started to blush.

What I really admired about Sally is that she handled her own horse and equipment even if she didn't own them. If she rode them, she took care of them, even though I was perfectly willing and capable of doing it for her. She seemed to take the same pride in her cowboying skills as I did in mine. And, she spoke her mind, although I often wondered just how outspoken she was.

Earlier in the day she seemed somewhat pensive, like she wanted to say something, but just didn't know how to go about it. I didn't give it much thought; I figured she would eventually come out and say it. But, if I remembered right, it had something to do with Dave and Marie's wedding.

As we walked from the barn to the house, with Sally holding

my hand, she said, "I sure wish you'd change your mind about the wedding, Honey, I had some big plans for it."

"Well, Darlin'," I said, "if it will make you feel better, I'll give it some further thought." I had heard my dad make this comment to my mother when she was trying to have him do something he didn't want to. It seemed to work. I hoped it would work this time.

Sally seemed to perk up as we walked to the house. *I wonder what's on her mind,* I thought.

After supper, Sally helped Mother with the dishes. I was in the living room watching television with Dad, Tommy, and Betty and could only hear parts of what they were saying. One of the parts I did catch was Sally saying, "Your son is so difficult to talk to sometimes. I had some things I wanted to say and just couldn't get the right answers from him."

Then I heard Mother say, "Did you have a nice ride? He seems to be more relaxed when he's horseback, not that he's uptight all the time. But he is comfortable when he's on a horse. I thought a ride might make it easier for you to discuss what you wanted to. I do know he's quite bashful and still quite shy."

I was straining to hear what they were saying, but couldn't catch it all.

My dad noticed this and asked, "Are you eavesdropping, son?"

"I guess so," I said.

"Leave 'em alone," he said. "Women need to talk a lot."

"Their conversation seems to be fairly serious, an' I think it's about me," I said.

"Don't let it bother you, unless you've done something to bother you. You haven't, have you?"

"No sir," I replied. "I think too much of her to even try anything funny." That was the truth.

"You keep it that way," said Dad. "At least until you are married," he added. He was very serious when he said that.

I was surprised when he added the "at least until you are married" part. Marriage—I hadn't given it any thought.

"Yes sir," I said, and I was very serious.

Dad continued talking and it was difficult for me to hear exactly what Sally and my mother were talking about. I thought that if Sally and I were alone again, I would ask her about this conversation with my mother. I really didn't think Sally had any problems expressing herself and, to me anyways, she didn't seem backward or shy.

When the dishes were done, Mother and Sally joined the rest of the family in the living room. Sally sat right beside me on the couch and immediately took my hand. I felt her squeeze it a little and it made me feel good. She seemed more relaxed and the serious look was gone from her face. She appeared to be herself, the Sally I knew and admired so much.

The next day was Sunday, Sally's last day. On Monday, I would take her to the bus station then go to school. I would be late for school, but I could handle it.

At breakfast, I asked Dad, "What do you have planned for today?"

"Just the normal chores. There's nothing pressing that needs to be done. Seeing as this is Sally's last day, why don't you two go for a nice long horseback ride? It's not too cold and the sun's shining. That might be a good thing. You can see how the fences are holding up."

I had no idea that this was just busy work, an excuse to let Sally and I have some quiet time together. It sounded like a job that needed doing and it gave me an opportunity to be with Sally.

"We can do that," said Sally, smiling. "It sounds like it's a worthwhile endeavor."

"I'll get saddled up," I said.

"And I'll saddle my own horse," said Sally. "This isn't a dude ranch and I'm certainly not a dude!"

We got saddled up and rode off.

"Check the bull pasture as you go out," said Dad, as we rode through the gate.

"You bet," I answered.

The ride to the bull pasture didn't take long. Sally was strangely quiet as we rode.

"What's on your mind? You're kinda quiet today," I said.

"This is my last day here and I really don't want to go back to school."

"I don't want to go back to school either," I said. "I do have a difficult time in school an' don't really enjoy it. I'll be glad to get out of it."

"I don't mind it so much," said Sally. "I really don't have a tough time in school. I just don't want to leave you."

Her statement caught me by surprise. I knew she thought a lot of me, but didn't know she wanted to be around me more. We hadn't done much during her visit, just regular ranch chores. We didn't alter our schedule to entertain her with anything special. We didn't even go to town to catch a movie at night. She seemed very content to sit around at night and visit with my family and slip down to the barn to practice our kissing.

Sally got that pensive, thoughtful look on her face again as we rode through the bull pasture. "Are you sure you won't go to the wedding with me?"

We had been through this the day before and I knew Sally was looking for a different answer than what I had given her yesterday. "I'll have to ask your dad about it and find out how much it costs," I said.

"Then you'll ask Daddy?"

"Yes," I said.

"When?"

"I suppose at Christmas time, when I go to your place," I said. "You still want to get together at Christmas, don't you?"

"Oh yes!" Sally almost yelled her answer. She seemed more relaxed and the pensive look disappeared from her face. Her questions seemed to be answered.

Our ride around the fences was leisurely. We didn't find any fence that needed fixing; consequently our ride was a nice visit with a lot of joking around. Occasionally, Sally would ask me a question I really didn't know the answer to or I didn't know how she wanted it answered. When this occurred, I would suggest we move the horses out a little. This gave me the opportunity to figure out an answer.

We returned to the house and I reported to Dad that the fences were all okay.

"I thought they would be," answered Dad. "How was your ride, little girl?" Dad had given Sally a new nickname and I think she liked it. I think my dad liked her.

"It was a very pleasant ride," answered Sally. "Very pleasant indeed!"

Supper that night was steak. "I thought you might be getting tired of leftover turkey," said my mother. "Being in the cow business, this is what we eat most all the time, beef. Although not always steak."

The next morning, we were all up early in preparation for Sally's departure. The plan was that I would take her to the bus station then go to school. I put Sally's bags in the back of my truck and after a tearful farewell between Sally and Mother, we left.

Sally was quiet on the way to town, and I drove a little faster than I needed to.

Sally asked, "Do we have to go this fast? You really want to get rid of me, don't you?"

"No, Darlin'," I said. "But if you miss the bus, then you'll miss your flight an' I'll be in some big trouble."

Sally grinned. "You'll be in bigger trouble if you stop calling me 'Darling'."

I could feel my face starting to heat up. I was blushing again.

"You're still my bashful, shy cowboy. Sometimes that makes it hard to be around you, but I like it anyway," said Sally.

At the bus station, we checked Sally's luggage and returned to my truck. We still had about half an hour before the bus left and we had some time to say goodbye. After a few kisses, Sally began looking for a handkerchief. I had a clean one and gave it to her. She was actually crying.

"I don't want to go," she said, wiping the tears from her eyes.

"I don't want you to go either. But it's what has to be done."

"Let's run away and get married! Then I won't have to leave you," cried Sally.

I was taken aback and didn't know what to say. "That might be a plan," I said. "But we really should plan this out."

"You'll talk to Daddy about the wedding, won't you?"

"I think when I come over for Christmas might be the best time," I said.

"Good! I'll see you then." One more kiss from Sally and she got on the bus. I watched her and she got a window seat, still wiping her eyes. She still had my handkerchief. *She's stealing my handkerchief,* I thought. *Oh well, I'll get it back at Christmas.*

The bus pulled out and I slowly drove to school, although my mind really wasn't on school. It had been a nice Thanksgiving holiday, although it had been much too short. Sally's presence gave me something to be thankful for. The upcoming Christmas vacation gave me even more to be thankful for.

A Slight Misunderstanding

The month or so between Thanksgiving and Christmas went slowly. School really didn't hold my interest and thoughts of Sally frequently entered my mind. Sally's letters arrived regularly and I couldn't wait for the vacation to start so I could see her again. Answering her letters once a week was not as exciting as having her around.

The week before school was to let out for Christmas break, I told my folks at supper, "I think I'll take my truck to school Friday, and then I can go straight to the Wilson's after school."

"We have another plan," said Mother. "You need to leave here early Saturday morning, pick up Sally at the airport, then drive to the Wilson ranch. We've already called Bud and he thinks that's a great idea and it will save him a trip to town."

"When did this plan develop? I haven't heard anything from Sally about it," I said.

"Sally has called me once a week since she left here," said Mother.

"She never told me," I said. "And how come I didn't get a chance to talk to her?"

"She called while you were in school and before you got home. She's in a different time zone, you know. She told me that, let's see … her exact words were, 'I don't want to distract him from his studies. I know it's real important that he graduate.' Yes, that's exactly what she said." Mother had a hard time saying that without coming right out and laughing.

"I didn't know you were talking to her on a regular basis," I said. "More regular than me!"

"That's all right," said Mother. "Sometimes women have things to discuss between themselves and men don't have any business meddling in such affairs!"

"That's absolutely right, son," said my dad. "And don't you ever forget it!"

On Saturday, when the holiday break began, I put my bed-roll in the truck, loaded my saddle and saddle blankets, made sure I had Sally's Christmas present in the box Clarence had given to me for it and got ready to go. I made a mental note to pick up some wrapping paper when I gassed up in town.

A kiss goodbye to Mother and a handshake with Dad and I was ready.

"It won't seem like Christmas without you this year," said Mother, as I gave her a hug. "But remember, you've been driving your present from your dad and me for more than a month."

"I remember," I said, "and I do really appreciate it. Have a merry Christmas!"

"You have a good Christmas!" Mother seemed a little sad as she said that. "And be sure to tell Sally I said Merry Christmas. Wait a minute—I have something for you to give Sally."

Mother left and Dad said, "Drive carefully. The roads might be slick and if you take your time, you'll get there. If you try to rush, you might not."

Mother returned with a Christmas gift for Sally. I started to put it in the back of the truck and Mother stopped me. "I'd put that in the front seat," she said. "It's special."

I put the package in the front and climbed in. A few more goodbyes and I was off. When I made it to town, I gassed up and went to the drug store to get wrapping paper and tape. I also picked up gift certificates for Bud, Pat, and the cook. I hadn't done any Christmas shopping for them.

That done, I headed for the bigger town about an hour and a half away and the airport. I had been told how to get to the airport and what time Sally's plane would arrive. I had her flight number and all I had to do was find out what gate her plane would be at. I figured I'd have about an hour to do that.

I thought I might wrap Sally's hackamore at the airport while I was waiting for her, but decided against it as I didn't have any scissors. As I drove the miles to the airport, I thought of how Sally must have felt when she rode the bus to our smaller town. Had she been as excited as I was getting?

I was at the gate when Sally's plane arrived. As she came down the ramp, she was yelling, "Honey! Honey!"

She ran up to me, threw both of her arms around me and started kissing. I had braced myself. Her greetings were similar to a football player getting tackled, although I managed to stay on my feet. However, I'm sure there's not as much kissing out on the football field as there was in the bus station before Thanksgiving or in the airport on this day.

I was starting to get used to these public displays of affection, but familiarity with them did not stop me from blushing. And my blushing got worse as I realized there were more people at the airport than at the bus station.

When she gave me a minute to catch my breath, I asked her, "Where's your luggage?" I really didn't want to stop the kissing, I just wanted to stop doing it in front of all the people. I did notice some smiles on stranger's faces as they watched us.

Sally led me to the baggage claim area. She had more bags this trip than what she brought to our place. When we got them outside the airport, I had Sally wait while I brought the truck around.

"What's this? My Christmas present?" Sally slid Mother's gift over as she got in.

"It's for you, from my mom. But don't you open it until Christmas. That's orders from my mother. Do you want to get something to eat?" I had the bags loaded. "You can tell me where there's a good restaurant; I'm not familiar with this town at all."

"There's a good place on the way to the ranch. Dad, Missus Abercrombie, and I have eaten there many times. It's good."

After another passionate kiss from Sally, we started out.

After we ate, we drove to the ranch, with Sally sitting as close to me as she could get. I followed Dad's instructions and didn't get in a rush. I was enjoying this.

We arrived at the ranch about an hour before supper. Sally had to give her dad a proper greeting, but not as proper as the one she gave me—she only kissed her dad on the cheek, but she kissed me all over my face. Pat also got a kiss on the cheek. I carried in the luggage with Pat's help. After the bags were put in Sally's quarters, I greeted Bud with a handshake.

"You're a little late," said Bud.

"My dad told me not to get in a big rush, so I just took my time," I said.

"Good thinking," said Bud.

I left Bud, Sally, and Pat to get reacquainted and took my bedroll to the bunkhouse. I would see if I could get a pair of scissors from the cook or Pat. I put Sally's hackamore under my bunk, figuring on wrapping it later. I also put the wrapping paper and tape under the bunk.

Sally came to the bunkhouse to get me for supper. It was good to see the cook again. After supper, we sat in the lodge in front of a fire and talked.

"Well, Honey," said Bud, "tell me how your folks are. I understand Sally's been talking with your mother on a fairly regular basis. Is everything okay there?"

"I guess so," I said. "I think Sally's talked to her more than I have. I didn't even know they were talking to each other until a few weeks ago."

"That's good," said Bud. "Your mother is like the mother Sally never knew."

I knew that Sally didn't have a mother, but didn't know the details. Had she died? Had her and Bud divorced? I didn't know, but thought better of asking, as I'd never heard it discussed.

"The folks are fine," I said. "They told me to tell you merry Christmas. So I've done that. Dad also told me to tell you about our new feedin' program. We started it last year and it worked good. Dad says he's goin' to do it again."

"What is it?"

"Dad got some literature on it and we tried it. It works! Rather than feedin' our cows in the mornin', we feed 'em at night, well, late afternoon. Then all the calves are dropped in the mornin'. Dad was real pleased with it; he says it saved him a lot of sleep. He's sold on it."

"That might be worth a try," said Bud.

"I've heard something about it," said Pat. "Now we have someone who's actually been involved with it. We need to pick his brain."

"Good luck," I said.

We all had a good laugh.

"Now," said Bud, "what's this I hear about a big wedding you've got planned?" Bud's face had a very stern, business-like look. I'd seen it before, when the bull had upended Sally's horse.

Pat's mouth dropped open and he had a surprised look on his face. Sally was behind her dad, smiling. The cook had started to leave, but stopped to listen. He had a surprised look on his face also.

"Go ahead Honey," said Sally. "Tell him."

"Yes," said Bud, "tell me." The look on Bud's face looked even more businesslike.

"Well," I said, "there's not much to tell. I was thinking that in June, Sally an' I might get some time off to go to a wedding. You see …"

Bud interrupted, "How old are you?"

"Seventeen," I answered. "I'll be eighteen in …"

Bud interrupted again. "Seventeen! You're not old enough!"

Sally said, "But Daddy …"

"You're not old enough either, daughter. Nope, you kids are much too young at this point. You've still got some growing to do, mentally, physically, emotionally, and perhaps even spiritually. Nope! While I might be in favor of the idea later on, not now. Why, you're not even out of school yet! And what are you going to do for a permanent job?"

I hadn't tried to interrupt Bud while he was talking, but I wasn't sure just what he was talking about.

"Well, sir, I was thinkin' I could work for you," I said. "It would only take a day or two to go to New Hampshire and …"

Bud interrupted again. "New Hampshire! If there's going to be any weddings around here, they're going to be done here. Why New Hampshire? We don't have any relatives back there, do we? It doesn't matter; you kids are still too young!"

"Daddy," said Sally, "this wedding is not for Honey and me; this is for Dave and Marie, although I wouldn't mind."

Sally looked at me in a peculiar, inviting way and smiled.

I was beginning to understand. Bud had thought I was asking to marry Sally!

"You mean you kids aren't getting married?" Bud looked straight at me when he said that. "You mean you don't want to marry my daughter?"

I was put on the spot. "Well, sir, I … ah … er … what I mean is … it's really okay if you say no."

Sally got me off the hook. "What Honey is asking is if we can go to Dave and Marie's wedding in June? That's all we want to know."

"Well," said Bud, "that's a different matter. I really thought you had other plans. What do you mean 'it's okay if I say no?' Don't you like Sally? I really thought you two had something together."

"No, ah … I mean, yes, I really do like your daughter." I was starting to get a little confused and felt like if I said anything at all, it would be the wrong thing.

The cook left, shaking his head, smiling and muttering to himself about "those crazy kids." Pat closed his mouth and regained his composure.

Bud laughed. "I guess I got the horse before the cart. I was all prepared for this moment, but I guess it was the wrong moment. However, we will all need to talk at some point in time. But, apparently, this is not the time. I'll need to see what's going on in June. We've got a pretty big summer lined up, dude wise, ah, that is guest wise."

We visited for a time, and then Sally took my hand and led me to the barn. It was kissing practice time. I thought I was getting pretty good, but didn't mind the practice at all.

After a kiss or two, Sally said, "How did you feel about our conversation with Dad?"

"I'll have to admit he seemed very confused. I even got a little tongue-tied myself."

"I can straighten things out with Daddy," said Sally. "How do you feel about his getting confused about us?"

"I thought it was a little strange," I said.

"No, no! I mean about us getting married!'

I felt like I was being put on the spot again and didn't exactly know what to say. I felt like I was being led into a trap, and I wasn't sure I wanted to get caught.

"I have given it some thought," I said. "You know we haven't even been dating, unless you want to call the hamburger I bought you at the hamburger joint at Thanksgiving a date. I kinda thought it was our first date. But," I continued, trying to change the subject, "Bud is right."

"What is Daddy right about, Honey? And what do you mean we haven't been dating? We've been together for all last summer, part of the summer before, and Thanksgiving and now Christmas. Doesn't all that count for something?"

"I really didn't know we were dating. I thought I was workin' for your dad. If I'd have known we were dating, I might have done things different."

"What would you have done different, Honey?"

"I don't know," I said. "I've never been on a date before. Maybe I could have cleaned up a little better." I was getting a little nervous. Sally could ask more questions than I thought possible. And I was having a hard time coming up with the right answers. She was quite blunt and I hadn't even considered some of the things she was talking about.

"Bud's just about right about everything, I guess. We ain't very old; my dad was over thirty when he got married. An' I do need a job."

"So you've thought about it?"

"Some," I said.

Sally seemed intent on pursuing this subject. I was glad we were in the barn with no lights. I was starting to blush again. I was almost wishing we could end this practice session early.

"Do you think that day will come, Honey?"

"What day?"

"Our wedding day," replied Sally.

I had to be careful here. I knew if I answered her wrong, I might be in for a lot of grief. If I could come up with the right answer, I might have an advantage.

"I don't know, Darlin'," I said. "We'll just have to see."

A little more practice kissing and I walked Sally to the lodge. I went to the bunkhouse and Pat was still up. Usually, he'd do a little reading then go to bed. But he was up tonight, like he was waiting for me.

I asked, "What do we have lined out to do tomorrow?"

"Not much, really. Just the feedin' then play with the colts some. I've been messin' with them some, but they're still a little distrustful. When's the weddin'?"

"Dave an' Marie are gettin' married in June. I don't know what day," I answered.

"No, no! I mean your weddin', you an' Sally's," said Pat.

"WHAT!?" I didn't know what to say.

It seemed to be a foregone conclusion, with everyone but me, as to what I was going to do before I did it.

"I don't think Bud would mind if you an' Sally got hitched," said Pat, "when you both get a little older. Why Bud has even said it would be like gettin' the son he never had. That's why Sally's so good at all the ranch jobs; she is tryin' to be not only a daughter, but also a son for Bud."

I asked, "You been drinkin'?"

"No," said Pat. "You know I don't touch the stuff. But with regard to Sally, just what are your intentions?"

"I really haven't given it much thought," I said. "So I just don't know."

I found myself wishing that I was a good conversationalist, so that I could direct a conversation rather than just answering these embarrassing questions. I knew that I was still lacking in the social graces.

Trying to change the subject, I asked, "You got any scissors?"

"Scissors? What do you need scissors for?"

"I need to wrap Sally's Christmas gift. Here, you want to see it?"

I pulled the box containing Sally's hackamore from under the bunk, took the hackamore out and held it up for Pat to see.

"Wow! That's about as fancy as you can get," he said, as he held it and inspected the braiding. "I'll bet that put you back a pretty penny."

"Think she'll like it?"

"I'm sure she will," said Pat. "But let me give you a few pointers. Women generally like other kinds of stuff; useless, worthless stuff that costs a lot of money, like necklaces, earrings, bracelets, and rings. Sally is sure to like that, but in the future, get her stuff she can't use, but likes to look at, or wear."

"If Sally don't like that, then I've sure got her judged wrong," I said. "Her horse can wear it." I said that like I knew a lot about women and knew what I was talking about. At least, that's what I wanted Pat to think. I was hoping that it would make as big a hit with her as the shirt I sent her last year, which I had bought by mistake.

Pat got some scissors and I wrapped the package. It wasn't a very professional job, but I hoped the contents would make a difference.

The next morning, after a leisurely breakfast, Pat and I did the feeding chores. When Bud and Sally came down to the corrals, we started to continue the education of the colts. I recognized most of them; I'd roped them when we branded them last spring. Pat had already started halter breaking them and most of them stood fairly well when tied. Those that fought a little got to stand tied longer. Pat, Sally, and I went to brushing the colts and picking up their feet.

"The more we do this now, the better they will become an' it'll be easier to break 'em to ride," said Pat. "Make sure you talk to each colt as you're messin' with 'em. That'll help a lot."

Sally didn't need any encouragement. "What do you want to do this afternoon, Honey?"

"I don't know," I answered. "What needs bein' done?"

"You might ride out through the cows, just to look," said Pat. "I've been ridin' through 'em every two or three days. Or you might ride through the broodmare bunch. We brought 'em up closer to the ranch for the winter. Won't be long before we'll have to start feedin'. Or you could ride through the weaners an' yearlings. But don't leave until we've finished here. The saddle horses are close, before lunch I'll saddle up an' run 'em in, an' you two can go after the noon meal."

"Sounds good to me," I said. "What direction do you want to go, Darlin'?"

Sally looked surprised when I called her "Darling" in front of Pat, but she didn't object.

I was kinda surprised, too. The name came real easy.

Pat was also surprised. His jaw dropped and he just stood there looking at me when I called Sally "Darling." Presently, he grinned and went back to what he was doing.

Sally asked, "Who do you want to ride, Honey?"

"I suppose Drygulch," I said. "Who are you goin' to ride?"

"I don't know," said Sally. "Dad's big paint needs the riding, but that's Dad's horse. I don't know how my horse, Beauty, is doing. I'd like to ride him, but he might buck me off."

"I'll top him off for you," I said. "He shouldn't be too bad, if we just handle him easy."

"But I wanted to be the only one to ride him," said Sally.

"That don't matter," said Pat. "Let Honey here top him off, an' you ride Drygulch. I'd feel better about it."

"I'll think about it during lunch," said Sally.

Pat ran the horses in while we ate and when we went out to the corral, he'd already put Sally's saddle on Drygulch. I put my saddle on the grulla that Sally called Beauty.

A rotten name for good lookin' horse like this, I thought, as I tightened the cinch. The horse stood and when I went to untrack him, he came apart. I jumped to the side as Beauty jumped straight up. I had the end of the mecate on my hackamore and held on to it as the horse bucked around me.

I asked Sally, "What ever prompted you to call this horse Beauty? I've got some other names that would fit him more appropriately, especially right now!"

"Are these names that can be used in public or mixed company?" she asked.

"Not really," I answered.

"Then he'll stay Beauty," said Sally.

I jerked on the mecate pretty hard a couple of times and the grulla stopped bucking.

"Better let me snub him for you," said Pat. He and Bud had finished eating and came to the corral.

"I can do that," said Sally, as she checked the cinch on Drygulch. She untracked him and climbed in the saddle.

Bud gave an approving nod, and I gave Sally the end of the mecate. "Take some good dallies," I said. "I don't think he's done."

Sally snubbed the horse up close; I put a foot in the stirrup and got on. I could feel the horse's muscles tensing up under the saddle.

"Start out easy, daughter," said Bud. He could see the horse was ready to buck again. "And keep it easy around the corral 'till he relaxes. He'll settle down in a little bit. He hasn't been ridden since you left for school, so don't rush him."

Sally led Beauty and me around the corral for about fifteen minutes. As we went around the corral, I told Sally to play out some more mecate. I wanted to do a little neck reining to see what the colt had forgotten and what he remembered.

Pat had a grin on his face. "How do you like bein' led around by a girl, Honey?"

"It's all right," I said, grinning. "But it's sorta dependant on where she's goin'.'"

"You ready to go outside?" Pat had moved to the gate and was ready to let us out.

"Soon as I put this mecate away," I said, as I took the mecate from Sally and tucked the end into my chap belt. "Let's go!"

Pat opened the gate and Sally and I rode out.

"Just make a short ride," said Bud. "We've got a few other things to do before supper and Christmas is just a few days away. We'll fix things so that we've only got minimal chores to do on that day and take a day off."

I waved an acknowledgement to Bud and Beauty shied and bucked a couple of jumps. He almost caught me off guard, but I pulled his head up and got him lined out. "Let's move these horses out an' work some of this energy out of him," I said, as I urged Beauty into a trot.

Sally spurred Drygulch into a trot and we trotted for about fifteen minutes. The horses were starting to breathe a little heavy so we slowed to a walk.

"I guess I should feel honored, you lettin' me ride your special horse," I said.

"Yes," said Sally, "you should. But you need to remember who led you around to start with!"

"I certainly will. But, I really don't trust this horse too much. He seems to be all right, but keep alert when you ride him. I think he'll need a lot of ridin' before he becomes trustworthy. I better ride him a few more times before you do."

Actually, I kinda enjoyed riding the horse. Sally had done a good job last summer teaching him neck reining and leg cues. The horse didn't fully trust anyone and he would only become trustworthy when people started trusting him. It would take time and a lot of riding.

I was thinking about this trust issue when Sally asked, "So, when's it going to happen?"

"It will take some time," I answered. "Developing trust doesn't happen overnight."

"You mean you don't trust me?"

Sally and I were having different conversations. I said, "What?"

"Don't you trust me?"

"Yes, I trust you, but what are you talking about?" I was becoming confused, as was often the case when I was with Sally. Despite the confusion, I enjoyed being around her.

"Us," she answered. "What are you thinking about?"

"I was just wondering about building up trust in this horse. I really don't know how to do it," I said. "It will take a lot of time before this horse becomes trustworthy."

"Oh," said Sally. "We were talking about two different things." She dropped the subject.

Actually, she was talking and I was thinking. I decided that I shouldn't let my mind wander when I was with Sally. I was going to pay more attention.

Christmas came, and after doing the morning chores, we all went to the lodge. We opened presents over an extra cup of coffee. I had slipped my present for Sally and my mother's present for Sally under the tree, along with the gift certificates I had picked up for Bud, Pat, and the cook.

The first present Sally picked to open was her present for me. It was about the size of a shirt and my first thought was, *She's returnin' the shirt I got for her, by mistake, last year.*

But it wasn't a shirt. It was a windbreaker jacket with the Wilson ranch logo on it. It also had my nickname, *Honey,* embroidered on it. It really looked pretty neat and it fit.

"I don't think I can wear this to school," I said.

"How come?" Sally had a very confused look on her face.

"Do you want everyone at my school calling me Honey?"

"I hadn't thought about that," she said. "You just wear it here."

Then, I gave Sally her present. I watched anxiously as Sally carefully opened it. I was remembering what Pat had said about buying women gifts that they could wear, and not necessarily use. I was very nervous.

Sally's mouth dropped open as she brought out the hackamore. "It's beautiful!" She carefully inspected the bosal, headstall, and mecate.

"I love it," she cried, as she came over and kissed me.

"I was afraid you might not like it," I said, giving Pat a triumphant look.

"Oh, I love it!"

Another kiss and I felt myself starting to blush. "Here," I said, trying to change the subject, "my mother sent this."

I handed Sally the package from my mother, which contained clothes, and Sally kissed me again for them.

"Give that to your mom, for me," she said. She kissed me again. "And your dad, too!"

Parting

The days after Christmas were spent riding around the ranch after the morning chores were done. Bud and Pat joined us on one occasion when we went out to check the broodmare band, but it was just Sally and I most of the time.

The first few days, I rode Sally's grulla, Beauty. Sally wanted me to use her new hackamore on the horse, but I declined.

"That's your hackamore, you use it," I said.

When we had decided that the grulla had been ridden enough that he wouldn't blow up, Sally rode him. She put her new hackamore on the horse and said, "Isn't it beautiful?"

The hackamore did look good on the horse. The colored strands of rawhide in the bosal really stood out against the shade of gray on the horse's head. And the black and white mecate made quite a contrast against the mouse-colored dun.

Sally and the grulla got along good during the next few days and our rides were leisurely and enjoyable. I paid close attention as we rode through the weaners and yearlings. I'd be breaking the yearlings the following summer when they were two year olds, if they were big enough. I was ready to get started now, but the time wasn't right.

Our discussions while we were riding were mostly directed by Sally and were about us. It almost seemed like she was trying to pin me down to something. I had an idea, but wasn't sure and was afraid to commit.

New Year's Eve didn't bring any special celebration at the ranch. At midnight, Pat fired a shotgun in the air, Sally gave me a big kiss, which I returned, the cook brought out some hot apple cider and Bud wished everyone the best for the New Year. It was pretty simple.

One evening, after supper, Bud asked me to have a talk with him. I was somewhat apprehensive about it; I wasn't sure just what he wanted to talk about.

"What's your plans after graduation? You are going to graduate, aren't you?"

"I expect to graduate," I said. "I'm lookin' forward to it. I'm not much of a student. I kinda thought I'd work for you this summer. After the summer, I don't know what I'll do."

"College isn't in your plans?"

"I don't think my grades are good enough to get into a college. I think the best learnin' is on the job rather than out of a book."

"You might be right there," said Bud. "You do exhibit an amazing amount of maturity, at times, for someone your age. But what about some specialized classes at the college level? Perhaps a two-year certificate of completion? How would you feel about that?"

"I hadn't given it any thought," I answered.

"I'm thinking some specialized classes might be helpful for you," said Bud.

"Like what?"

"Well," said Bud, "I've been thinking about our new replacement heifer program. We might build a facility here to feed out the replacement heifers and breed them artificially here. It's kind of expensive having those heifers I bought from your dad in a feedlot. I'd need someone to do that, rather than having some-one come out from town everyday to do it. If you were inclined, you could work here year round, learn how to artificially insemi-nate and help us out that way. We'd still have the dude business during the summer, the colts to mess with year round, and our everyday chores.

"You seem to do all right with the stuff we've been doing here and I'm very pleased with your performance. In fact, if you don't want to work here, even though I want you to, I'd certainly give you a good job recommendation if you want."

"Are you offerin' me a year-round job?"

"Yes. Do you think I'm just killing time with an extra cup of coffee after supper?"

We both laughed.

"I'd need to think about it," I said. "I don't know what my dad's plans are."

"Of course," said Bud. "You talk it over with your dad, see what he says. Remember, you do have a job here, year round if you want it."

"Yes, sir." I said. "And thank you. You know I'll be here in the spring an' I'll be prepared to give you an answer then."

"That's good enough for me," said Bud. "Now what are your plans with Sally?"

"I've been thinking about it some," I said. "Sally's been kinda persistent about something, although she hasn't come right out and said anything about it. I just …"

Bud interrupted, "Of course! Ladies don't come out and ask men to marry them until leap year, and that's a ways away yet, and I raised Sally to be a lady. She has talked with me about you and you have given her some problems! I'm not sure just how to answer her or help her."

"I'm glad to hear I'm givin' her some problems," I said. "I thought I was the only one havin' problems!"

Bud laughed, but I was serious. Sally had certainly given me some problems, although it was sorta nice.

"I suppose I'll have to talk to her," I said.

"That would be a good idea," said Bud, laughing. "And be ready to be welcomed into the family in a couple of years! But don't get into a big rush! You two are still pretty young yet."

I didn't know what to say.

The next day we went riding. It was our last day together. We both had to leave for school the following day.

As we left on our ride, Sally asked, "How was your Christmas break? You know we'll have to go back to school."

"I think this was probably the best Christmas I've ever had," I said. "And you certainly helped make it that way."

"So you like your windbreaker?"

"Yes, but you didn't have to get me anything. I was perfectly contented enjoyin' your company," I said.

"I wanted to get you something so you'd remember me. I thought the windbreaker with our logo on it might do the trick."

Little did she know that she was in my thoughts almost constantly. I was just going to say something about thinking about her was the reason my grades weren't all that good, but decided against it. My grades had never been that good, even before I met her.

I was concerned. She sounded like she wasn't coming back. "You mean you're not coming back?"

"Not until after school's out, silly."

"Do you know your dad offered me a year-round job?"

"Yes," said Sally, "I put him up to it!"

"You mean you bribed your dad into offerin' me a full-time job?"

"No, Honey. I put the idea in his head last summer. He said he'd think about it and make a decision. I guess he's made his decision. What did you tell him? Yes, I hope." Sally's face had a look of expectation on it.

"I told your dad that I'd have to talk to my dad. I don't know what his plans are." I was watching Sally closely as I answered her.

At my answer, she frowned a little, then again became positive, as she asked, "You mean there's a chance you might stay after the summer and work year round?"

"Well, yes," I said. "Other than workin' for your dad next summer, I ain't made no plans. What are your plans?"

"If you're working here, I will be here, too" said Sally.

"Then what?"

"I want to be where you are, wherever you are," she replied.

I was stunned. I couldn't believe it. In disbelief, I asked, "What?"

"That's right, Honey," she answered. "Wherever you are."

"What does that mean?"

"Can't you see, stupid? I love you! I don't know what I'd do without you."

"But," I said, nervously, "we're not together durin' the school months."

"The thought of seeing you again in the spring is the only thing that keeps me going. It's really hard to concentrate, thinking of you."

I was glad I hadn't said anything about my grades suffering because of her, but was surprised to learn how our thinking was so similar.

She leaned out of the saddle to give me a kiss, but her grulla horse shied at the movement. She didn't fall off, but abandoned the kissing idea as she regained her seat.

She laughed. "I'll finish that when we get back to the ranch," she said.

"You're dad also asked me what my plans were with you," I said.

Sally looked serious again. "What did you tell him?"

"I told him I'd have to talk to you," I said.

"What did he say?"

"He said somethin' about gettin' ready to be welcomed into the family in a couple of years. I don't know exactly what he meant, I guess I'll have to ask him," I said.

"That means he approves! He's already consented. Yes!" Sally had a big smile on her face and at the same time she looked like she was ready to break out in tears.

I didn't know what to say or do.

"Let's move these old broomtails out a little," I said, as I spurred Drygulch into a fast lope. Moving the horses out a little faster was becoming my way of getting out of uncomfortable situations. Sally squealed and spurred Beauty. She wasn't long in catching up and soon we were running the horses side by side.

Sally put out her hand to me and instinctively, I took it. It was an exhilarating feeling as we ran the horses. After a while, we stopped and Sally kissed me. Her horse was a little winded and he didn't even shy.

"I guess that settles it," said Sally.

"Oh, what's settled?"

"Now we're officially betrothed," said Sally.

I asked, "What does that mean?"

"Now we're engaged," said Sally, smiling. "I thought it would take longer than this. You're really quite the Casanova, Honey!"

Sally leaned over to kiss me again. When we were done, I said, "But, ah … don't we need a ring to be, ah, engaged?"

"Not me Honey! This is good enough for me!"

"Doesn't a guy have to get down on one knee to do that?

We're still horseback!" I was kinda nervous and not one hundred percent sure of what was happening.

"That's the way it should be for us. That one knee stuff is just in the movies and you're too shy and bashful to do that anyway. If I had to wait for you to do that, I could become an old maid!"

Sally was pretty enough that I was sure she wouldn't become an old maid.

"But I thought you needed a ring," I said.

"Don't worry about that," said Sally.

I was quiet riding back to the ranch, contemplating what had happened. Sally didn't notice, she was busy talking about all the things we were going to do together as a couple. I listened, and it didn't sound all that bad, but I still had some misgivings about the deal.

We got back to the ranch, unsaddled our horses, and turned them loose. Sally gave me a big kiss. "You've made me very happy," she said.

"I suppose you're goin' to tell everyone."

"Certainly," said Sally.

"But you don't have anything to prove it with," I said.

"That's okay. I don't need to prove it, I know it!"

"Well, here," I said, taking off the neckerchief I had around my neck. "You wear this. It's just like a ring." I tied the neckerchief loosely around her neck and while I was doing it, she kissed me again.

As we walked up to the lodge, I thought, *She must be the kissin' champ in the country. I wonder if her lips are chapped.* I made a mental note to check.

At supper, Sally proudly announced, "We're engaged!"

The cook started to choke on his mouthful of food. Pat's mouth dropped open and he almost missed it with a forkful of food. I blushed.

Bud got up, slapped the cook on the back a couple of times

to help him get his food down, reached for my hand, shook it, and said, "So when's the big day?"

"We haven't decided yet," said Sally. "But we'll let you know!"

"Good," said Bud. "But it had better be a couple of years down the road, you two are pretty young yet. Long engagements are the best. But when the big day does arrive, we'll do it right here, and we'll do it up right! Congratulations, Honey! Maybe that means I can stop calling you Honey and start calling you son!"

"Congratulations, Honey," said Pat.

The cook was busy catching his breath and didn't say anything.

That night, sleep came kinda tough and it wasn't real peaceful. Had I done the right thing? I certainly hadn't done it the right way, or at least what I thought was the right way.

The next morning during breakfast, I told Bud that I'd be at the ranch the day after graduation.

"That'll be fine," he said. "Be sure and bring your saddle horse and your donkey."

"You bet," I said. "You ready, Darlin'?"

"Yes," said Sally. A quick kiss on her dad's cheek, a kiss to the cook and Pat, and she got in the truck. I put my saddle and bedroll in the truck, loaded up Sally's stuff and we headed to the airport.

I drove slowly to the airport. We had plenty of time. Sally just beamed all the way. She was very happy. I was thinking, *How do you act when you're engaged? How do I tell my folks? What do I do?*

"Your awfully quiet," said Sally. "What's on your mind?"

"I've never been engaged before," I said. "I'm not sure I know how to act."

"Just be your sweet, loveable self."

"I guess this bein' engaged means I will have to stop flirtin' with all the other girls, huh?"

"Ha! You've never flirted with any girls," said Sally.

"How did you know?" I let that slip out and didn't mean to. I started to blush.

"I can tell," laughed Sally. She was enjoying this. "And your mother told me."

We arrived at the airport with plenty of time to spare. After some kissing practice in the parking lot, we checked her luggage.

"Do you want somethin' to eat? If we got a hamburger, it would be our second date," I said.

"You're really on a roll, aren't you?" Sally was laughing again. "We've been dating every time we're together! Didn't you know that?"

"I guess not, but you're a pretty cheap date," I said. "I haven't spent a dime on you at the ranch."

"I'll bet you spent plenty on that hackamore you gave me for Christmas and the blouse you gave me last year!"

"Don't forget the hamburger I bought you when you came out for Thanksgiving an' the hamburger I got you a week ago," I was teasing her a little. It was all right, she did it to me all the time.

"So, you're independently wealthy, huh?"

"I certainly am," I said. "Why, I've even got money I ain't spent yet!"

We got something to eat and then waited for her boarding time. When her flight was announced, a long kiss was in order, and I was blushing when she left for the gate.

"Good job, young man," someone said. We had been watched and I felt like I could slug the feller that had said that. But I didn't know who it was. Everyone was smiling or grinning.

Sally waved as she entered the plane. I waited around until the plane taxied out to the runway, then went to my truck. I really did feel sad, and wasn't in a rush to get home. I took my time.

I got home and was welcomed with a big hug from my mother. "How are the Wilson's? How was your Christmas? How is Sally?"

I was wondering if it wasn't in the female makeup to ask a lot of questions. "The Wilson's are fine," I replied. "Christmas was fine and Sally's engaged." I didn't mean to let the last part slip out.

Mother looked surprised. "Who's she engaged to?"

"Well," I said, "ah … me, I guess."

"Oh, really! How did this come about?" Mother looked a little shocked.

"I'm not sure," I said. "It just happened."

"Where did you get the ring and when?"

"I didn't have a ring," I said.

"What did you give her?"

"I tied my neckerchief around her neck," I said.

"That's very romantic," said Mother. A faint smile entered her lips. I thought she might be thinking of a six- or seven-year-old kid's first puppy love. "So when's the big day?" Mother had regained a little of her composure.

"I don't know," I said. "Sally hasn't decided."

Mother looked a little more relieved. "You'll invite us to the wedding?"

"Certainly," I said. "You an' Sally can plan it, if you want."

"I'll write her about it," said Mother. "We have been corresponding quite a bit as of late. This will give us quite a bit to talk about."

"Of course," I said, "Missus Abercrombie will want to have a hand in it. Her an' Sally are quite close."

"Put your stuff away. Your dad and Tommy and Betty will be coming in soon. We do have some presents for you to open. You can do that after supper."

"I really don't need anything," I said.

"They're leftovers from Christmas. We can't take them back, so you're stuck with them," said Mother.

Dad took the news of my engagement well, preferring to remain silent until a definite date was set. He did make the remark, "You two are pretty young."

All the older folks seemed to think we were pretty young.

Graduation

I went back to school the next day. I really wasn't too excited about it, but pleased to know it would all be over in June. I felt good, but had some lingering doubts in my mind about being engaged.

We resumed the procedure we started last January, feeding in the evenings so the calves would come during the morning hours. Dad would load the hay in the morning, and then Tommy and I would help him feed after school. The horses had been turned out and they were fed after we fed the cattle. The cows would start calving in March and there wasn't much to do other than the regular chores.

I received letters from Sally once a week and I would answer them the following day during study hall in school. I would mail them from school. I was surprised at Sally's letters; they had taken on a more personal note since our engagement. I shouldn't have been surprised, Sally was always outspoken.

January and February seemed to drag by. Toward the end of February, we brought in the saddle horses to prepare for calving. After the calving started, we would rope the calves and ear tag them. Dad would generally wait until the weekend so Tommy and I could get in on the roping. I really looked forward to the roping on the weekends.

I wondered how Roman would act when I saddled him up for the first time this year. Last year he acted like he might be inclined to buck a little. The first Saturday after the calving started and after the feeding was done, I saddled Roman and got ready to top him off. I was surprised when he didn't even offer to buck and walked right out just like the good horse he was.

The roping was a little difficult. Both Tommy and I missed a lot of throws; Dad was the only one that caught calves consistently. But then, he'd had a lot more practice than us kids. Dad was real pleased with the evening feeding as opposed to morning feeding. The biggest percentage of the calves were born around six o'clock in the morning or later. This allowed Dad a little more sleep each night and he was in better spirits most of the time.

When we were about done calving, we made preparation for branding. A lot of relatives and friends were invited, and our home ranch resembled a campground, with tents and camp trailers parked all over. The main talk among the visitors was my impending marriage and I took a lot of guff from my relatives about it.

The most commonly asked question was, "Are you going to invite us to the wedding?"

My stock answer was, "I don't know. Sally's in charge of the invitations."

My mother's answer was, "My son is much too shy and bashful to have a big wedding and a date hasn't been set yet."

My dad's answer was, "I don't know."

I was really glad when the branding started. The questions, which seemed endless, melted away in favor of roping, dragging calves to the fire, and the work associated with the process. My roping hadn't improved much and I was preoccupied with details of the wedding and how Sally would react to my report of my relative's response. Did she want a big wedding?

Our branding took two days and when we finished around

midday on the second day, we trailed the cattle to the outside fence on the way to the summer range. A big barbeque was ready when we returned to the ranch house. A close friend had not helped with the branding at all, but stayed in the front yard at the house and did the cooking.

The meal was fantastic and I thought it was almost as good as the cook at the Wilson's had done.

I was relieved when the friends and relatives left. I had been the center of attention over the weekend and was very uncomfortable during the whole affair. I was still lacking in my social skills. I didn't know what to do about this; I was fairly comfortable as I was. But I wasn't used to being the center of attention. Sally and Bud had reassured me during the previous summer that I was doing well with the tourists, but I wasn't doing anything other than being myself. Being myself appeared to be the best way to go, although it might be a little difficult at times.

Having turned the cattle out, the daily feeding chores were finished. New chores, such as irrigating became paramount. I didn't think much of these farming chores, preferring to do the cattle work from horseback. The horses were turned into the horse pasture and Betty brought Sassy to the corrals close to the house. She had been playing with Sassy during the previous summer and she decided that she wanted to break the donkey to ride.

I asked, "Why do you want to ride a donkey?"

"I think it would be cute in the 4-H parade."

I didn't have a reply, but went down to the corral to watch my sister ride her burro. I wasn't sure just what would happen, but wanted to be around just in case Betty needed my help.

I shouldn't have worried. Betty saddled Sassy, climbed aboard and rode off. The donkey acted like she'd done it a thousand times. I was surprised.

"How come that donkey has acted so good?"

"Because she's my donkey," replied Betty. "And I've done a lot of work with her."

"What kind of work?"

"I taught her to drive last summer," answered Betty. "She already knows just about all she needs to know."

I left Betty and Sassy and went to check on Matilda. She'd been turned out with the saddle horses all winter and other than looking at her when we fed, she hadn't received any attention. She was in good shape, although she hadn't shed her winter coat as nicely as the horses. I got her halter and led her to the barn, where I started brushing her. She would certainly need to look a lot better for the guests at the Wilson's.

As I brushed the donkey, I thought about my plans. I was scheduled to graduate on a Saturday; I'd already rented my cap and gown. I failed to see the need for such attire, but was informed it was necessary. The graduation ceremony would take all day, and I thought I would leave Sunday morning for the Wilson's.

According to Sally's letters, she would be arriving at the ranch about a week after I did. Her graduation ceremony wouldn't take place until a week after mine. Bud was going to fly back and be present for her graduation, and they would come to the ranch together.

My graduation day finally arrived. I felt silly in the cap and gown I was wearing and even sillier listening to all the speeches about how this graduating class was going to change the world. I was pleased to know that the diplomas were going to be handed out in alphabetical order rather than by class ranking. That would mean I would be in the middle, towards the first, rather than towards the end.

My name was called, and I walked across the stage, took my diploma, shook the principal's hand, and walked back across the stage, tapping my diploma in my open hand. *Finally,* I thought, *Finally!*

I was free. I didn't have any obligations, other than to Bud and, of course, to Sally. I didn't have any real plans, other than to work for the Wilson's on a year-round basis. Things just seemed to be coming together.

Graduation night, when all the other graduates were out dancing and partying, I was packing my stuff. I thought I would need more than I had needed previous years; I was going to be gone all year.

The morning after graduation, I loaded my clothes, bedroll, and such into the truck.

"Better put as much of that stuff in the front as you can get," said Dad. "You don't want your animals crapping all over it in the back."

"Good idea," I said, embarrassed that I hadn't thought of it myself. I cinched my saddle on the side rack and cinched it down fairly tight so the saddle blankets underneath it wouldn't blow away. Then I loaded Roman and Matilda and tied them to the rack in front. I was ready to leave.

I drove the truck to the house to say goodbye to my family.

"I don't know when I'll see you again," I said.

"I know, son," said Mother. "But you keep in touch. We didn't hear from you very often last summer and you need to write more often. I don't know that we can get away this year to visit you like we did last summer."

"I know," I said.

Kisses to Mother, a kiss to Betty, a handshake to Dad and Tommy, and I was ready.

"Be sure to give the Wilson's our best," said Mother, as I got into the truck.

"You bet," I said. I drove out of the yard. I was on my own.

I didn't know it, but Mother and Dad had a conversation about me after I left.

"I don't know when we'll see him again," said Mother.

"That's true," said Dad. "But don't worry about him. He's been grown up for some time now. He's a man and he'll be all right. Sometimes I think he was born very mature."

"Yes," said Mother, "but he's still my son."

I drove along, unaware of Mother and Dad's conversation. I was anxious to get to the Wilson's. I stopped in town to get gas and looked for a ring to get Sally, but all the jewelry stores were closed as it was Sunday. I was concerned—where could I get a ring on Sunday?

As I drove on, I considered the problem. Sunday was a poor day to shop for jewelry. Then, I hit on an idea. The airport! The shops at the airport were open every day and I should be able to find something there. My plan being formulated, I decided to go to the airport.

The parking attendant at the airport gave me a funny look as I pulled in.

"You got tickets for them?" He was looking at my animals in the back of the truck.

"No," I said, somewhat irritated. "But I only need one ticket. They're goin' to sit in the same seat. Are the shops in the airport open today?"

"Yep."

"Don't let anybody mess with my animals, truck, or stuff while I'm inside."

"Yes, sir!"

I noted the sir and the emphasis on it, and even relished a little in it. After all, I was a graduate, a man, set out on his own. I thought I should get used to it. I failed to recognize the humor and ridicule in the attendant's comment.

I parked the truck close to the parking attendant's station, and went into the airport to look for a jewelry store. I didn't know what size to get but figured just about anything would do. We could get it fitted at a later date. In the jewelry store, I was greeted with some skepticism, but a nice lady consented to help me.

"I need an engagement ring," I said.

"Do you know what you want? There are lots of styles to choose from," said the saleslady.

"I really don't know much about it," I said. "I don't want one too fancy, she's a working girl. I don't want it to get in the way of her work."

The saleslady smiled slightly. "Let me show you these."

The lady brought out a tray of rings. "These are moderately priced and are of exceptional value. What size do you need?"

"I don't know," I said. "How do you figure that out?"

"Tell me about your lady," said the clerk.

I was beginning to blush. "She's mighty pretty, about this tall." I held my hand up to where Sally's head came on my shoulder. "And she's kinda slim."

"Hold out your hand," said the clerk.

"What for, I ain't goin' to wear it."

"I know a little trick. Let's see your hand."

I held my hand out and the lady slipped a ring on one of my fingers. It slid on pretty easily and she took it off and tried another one. I felt real foolish, but the lady didn't give me a chance to complain. After a few tries, she finally selected one.

"This one might do the trick," she said.

"How can you tell?"

"It's a trade secret, and it's quite accurate. If it doesn't fit properly, you'll have ninety days to bring it back for exchange. If you need to make some adjustments, bring your young lady in for a proper fit. And bring in your sales slip."

"I'll take it," I said.

The saleslady didn't seem at all surprised when I paid her cash for the ring. "Be sure to bring her in when you're ready to select a wedding ring!"

"Yes, mam," I said. I carefully put the ring, in its case, in my pocket and left.

When I got to the truck, there was a family of five kids and the mom and dad admiring my horse and burro. They wanted to know if they could ride them, but there wasn't a place to unload at the airport. Matilda would have plenty of that later during the summer.

I leisurely drove to the Wilson ranch. There wasn't a need to hurry because Sally wouldn't be there for about a week.

I arrived at the Wilson ranch and was surprised to find nobody there. I unloaded Roman and Matilda and turned them out in the horse pasture, then unloaded my stuff in the bunkhouse. I went to the lodge and found the cook preparing the evening meal.

"We figured you'd be here sometime today, Honey," said the cook. "You want some coffee?"

"Nope," I said. I'd quit drinking coffee after noon as it tended to keep me awake at night. "Where's everybody?"

"Bud went back east to Sally's graduation an' Pat's out gatherin' some cattle. He should be back shortly. Just take it easy here an' tell me what's been goin' on."

I sat in the kitchen and visited with the cook until Pat showed up. After a handshake and a greeting, Pat said, "We've got some work to do tomorrow, Honey. There's a piece of fence down that'll need fixin'. I think I've got the cattle put back, but we'll have to fix fence then ride the country an' look for any cattle that I may have missed. We can take the truck to fix fence, we'll need wire, stretchers, staples, and such, then come back an' get the horses to look for the cattle. We can do it after the mornin' chores."

"Sounds good to me," I said, although I didn't really like the idea of fixing fence. "Where do you want me to park my truck? I don't figure I'll be needin' it much all summer."

"It's okay where it is for now. You can park it out of sight before the dudes arrive."

I took offense at Pat's remark about putting the truck out of sight, but didn't say anything. I didn't really think my truck was an eyesore. We visited for a spell, hashing out the old times and discussing the upcoming summer dude season. It appeared that the summer was going to be pretty busy with the dudes. Before we turned in for the night, I put Sally's ring in the jockey box of my truck. I didn't want to lose it out fixing fence.

There wasn't much to the morning chores and soon we were headed out to fix fence. There was a big stretch of fence down and it took all morning to fix it.

"How did this happen?" I was curious.

"I don't know," said Pat. "Could have been elk run through it or some mustangs got in a fight an' tore it up. Could have been anything. There's all kinds of tracks around here. We might find out when we look for any cattle I might have missed."

I let Pat's comments rest and applied myself to fixing fence. I always thought the quicker I finished an unpleasant job, the sooner I would be done with it.

When we finished, Pat said, "Horse high, hog tight, an' bull strong. That'll hold 'em, for a while anyways."

We went back to the ranch, had a noon meal and saddled our horses to hunt for any cattle Pat may have missed the day before. I rode Roman and Pat was on his private horse. We didn't find any cattle, but spotted a lone horse out on the flats. About a mile to the south, we spotted a small bunch of horses.

"That's probably our culprits," said Pat. "Mustangs."

"We ought to run 'em in or run 'em off," I said.

"We can try an' corral 'em. There's a big corral off to the

west. You know it, Honey, it's where we brand. I'll see if I can sneak around 'em an' lead 'em to the corral. You follow, but not to close, an' make sure we don't spill any of 'em. Give me some time to get ahead of 'em then bring 'em. Try to get that lone horse. He's probably a stud that got whipped. He might readily follow the others.

"It'll take me about half an hour to get in position. When you see me top that little rise, bring 'em. You can work your way around that lone horse, but keep me in sight as much as possible."

I watched Pat ride off, taking his time. I slowly circled around the lone horse and soon topped a little rise where I could keep both Pat and the lone horse in sight. The lone horse was slowly grazing toward the small bunch of horses. There were only five or six horses in the bunch and Pat wasn't having any problem getting around them unnoticed.

When I figured Pat was ready, I started the lone horse moving in the direction of the other horses. As the lone horse approached the others, a horse came out to meet him. *Probably the other stud,* I thought.

The other horses followed Pat and I hurried the lone horse to the others. The horse that came out to meet us saw me and instantly turned back toward the horses that were following Pat. The lone horse followed.

We had to do this from a distance. If we'd have gotten too close to the wild horses, they'd have scattered in all directions. Pat rode right into the corral and I rushed the bunch so we could corral them all. When I got to the gate, I brought Roman to a sliding stop, jumped off and closed the gate. We had our wild horses.

"Better come in here, Honey," said Pat. "We need to separate the two studs or they'll fight all night."

I took Roman into the corral, closed the gate, and mounted.

"We'll rope each stud an' put him in a separate corral. While we've got 'em in a different corral, we'll heel 'em, stretch 'em out, an' cut 'em."

I roped one stud and dragged him, with Pat encouraging him from the rear, to another pen. Pat roped the hind legs, half-hitched his rope to the horn, got off and took out his knife.

"Will your horse hold him?" I knew Pat would be in a dangerous position if the stud got his hind legs free.

"Yeah. He'd better!"

Pat cut the end of the scrotum, exposing the stones. Then he pulled some hair from the tail of the horse and tied off the cords.

"Make sure you get the buttons," I said. "We don't need any proud cut geldings runnin' around here."

Pat nodded his head and grinned. "We'll do the job right!"

When the job was done, Pat took his rope off the head and got back on his horse. The ex-stud just laid there for a minute. Pat hit him with the end of his rope and the horse stood up.

"I wish we had some antibiotic to use. It would be nicer and cut down the risk of infection. He could use some on those other wounds, either caused by a fight or the fence they took out."

We roped the other stud and performed the same operation. This horse had a big bite on his neck and the flesh was hanging down, exposed to the elements and the dirt.

"Maybe we'll bring some medicine back and doctor these animals," said Pat. "We'll need to bring some hay an' a couple of water troughs. We'll just keep them here until Bud shows up an' decides what to do with 'em. They're not an outstanding bunch of horses. He'll probably just run 'em through the sale."

"When's Bud an' Sally showin' up?"

"He should be here in less than a week," answered Pat. "He'll be bringin' Missus Abercrombie and Sally. I thought you'd never ask about Sally!"

"She wrote me an' told me what the plan was," I said.

"Then you know more about what's goin' on than I do," said Pat.

It felt good to be one up on Pat. He was pretty much aware of everything that went on around the ranch.

"So, what's your plans with Sally? When's the big day?"

"I dunno, she hasn't told me yet," I replied.

"Maybe I should ask, what's Sally's plans with you?"

"Either way," I said, "she hasn't told me yet."

Pat laughed. "I suppose she will, when she's ready. We better go back and get some hay and the water troughs. I hate to just leave the hay out. The elk an' deer will get it, an' maybe some cows. I don't know how we'll store the hay here, though."

"This must be your lucky day," I said. "You're really fortunate I showed up. I just happen to have a ready made enclosure for hay storage an' it's ready to go."

"Huh?" said Pat.

"My truck," I said. "We can load the hay on it, bring it out here an' leave it until the horses go to the sale. I sure ain't plannin' on goin' anywhere. Besides that, didn't you say somethin' about hidin' the truck?"

"That's an idea," said Pat. "Honey, you're a genius. I think we'll do it. We can ride out here an' feed an' water once a day. Good idea!"

We rode back to the ranch, loaded my truck with hay and a couple of water troughs and I drove it to the corrals. Pat followed in a company truck. We set the troughs in place and Pat turned on the water taps. Water had been piped to the corrals some years earlier.

"We'll have to fill these each day. I don't have any float valves for 'em. These troughs should stay here all the time. We just bring 'em in during the winter so they won't fill up with water an' freeze."

I parked the truck outside the corrals, locked the doors, and we headed back to the ranch in the company truck.

"So, when's the big day? I'm thinkin' this outfit could use a little excitement," said Pat.

"You know Sally ain't told me yet," I said.

"Sounds like to me, Sally's gonna wear the pants in this family! I wonder how that will work out. How do you feel about it?"

I hadn't really given any thought to being boss in the future and didn't know what to say. Before I could answer, Pat continued, "Don't get in any big rush about this. You're both pretty young yet an' there's plenty of time to figure out these little details. Hah!" He laughed as he made the last remark.

I was prepared to listen to another lecture on being too young, but Pat didn't say anything else. He just grinned and laughed all the way back to the ranch.

We had put in a pretty good day, and decided to do the evening chores and get supper.

Pat lined me out during supper on what we were supposed to do until Bud showed up. Besides the morning chores and having to feed the wild horses we'd corralled, we needed to ride fence and make whatever repairs were necessary. If we had time, we could gather the yearlings and two year olds, and start playing with the two year olds. These were the colts I was going to start riding during the summer. Some of the part-time summer help might start showing up, and we could help them get settled.

Reunion

"Who's coming for summer help? Anybody I know?" I was curious as to who might show up from last year. I was certain Dave and Marie wouldn't make it because they were getting married. I wasn't sure about Jim and Jeff or Linda and Josie.

"I'm not sure," said Pat. "I think Jim is coming back, he fit real well into the head housekeeping roll last year. I don't know if Jeff is coming back. As for the girls, I don't know. Tomorrow, we'll start ridin' fence."

"Good," I said. "We can use Matilda to carry fence stretchers and such, if you've got a pack saddle that'll fit her."

"Don't have a pack saddle that will work, but we can use the kid's saddle that we used on her last summer. We can put the tools in gunny sacks an' tie them on. We might get this job done quicker than I thought."

The next couple of days were spent fixing fence. One day, Jim showed up. He had spent the previous summer as the head housekeeper because he really couldn't ride.

Jim got settled in and went right to work, starting to fix up the guest accommodations. A day later, Josie showed up.

I had thought Jim and Josie had something going on from the previous summer, but they didn't show it, at least they didn't show it like Sally showed it to me!

At supper that night, Josie said, "We understand there are

some big things going on between you and Sally, Honey." Josie wanted to satisfy her curiosity. "When's the big day?"

I was starting to feel flushed. "I ain't sure. Sally ain't told me."

Pat said, grinning, "Sally's goin' to be boss in that family!"

"Well, she's told me plenty," said Josie. "We corresponded all winter, you know, and quite a bit of it was about you!"

"Me?"

"Yes, you! You certainly have her infatuated with you. How did you do it?"

"I dunno," I said. I really hadn't intended to do anything, I had just been myself. "Did you girls spend all winter writing about me?"

"Not all winter, but you were the main topic of conversation from Sally. There wasn't hardly a letter go by that didn't say how much she missed you and how she couldn't wait until school was out and you could be together."

"Really," I said. I was blushing and surprised that I would be the main topic of conversation between two girls.

Trying to change the subject, I said, "I understand Dave an' Marie are gettin' married this summer."

"Yes," said Jim. "And our band will be shot without a fiddle player. Are you going to the wedding?"

"No," I said. "I don't see as how I can get away, with all the colts that have to be rode." Actually, I really didn't want to go, although Sally was in favor of going. "Is Jeff coming back?"

"Jeff will be here in a day or two. Maybe the two of us can still provide some music for the dances, although it won't be the same without a fiddle."

The next day, Pat and I completed riding fence. We'd ridden the whole ranch and even caught a glimpse of the broodmare band one day.

"We'll be runnin' them in when Bud an' Sally get here," said Pat, as we turned our horses back toward the ranch.

A day later, Jeff showed up. The following day, Linda showed up driving a yellow convertible with the top down. The sight of the car seemed to confirm my suspicions—a little rich girl.

The next day, Bud, Sally, and Missus Abercrombie were supposed to arrive. They hadn't arrived by suppertime and after supper Pat, the cook, and I sat up making small talk waiting for them to arrive. When they hadn't arrived by ten o'clock, Pat decided it was time to hit the sack. I agreed with him and we both turned in. The cook said he'd wait up for 'em.

Jeff and Jim were already in bed when Pat and I got to the bunkhouse.

"Where's Bud and Sally?" The question was simultaneous from both of them. "When will they be here?"

"Don't know," said Pat. "They'll be here when they get here. Go to sleep; we've got a big day tomorrow."

I climbed into bed and it wasn't long before I was asleep.

Sometime later, I was awakened by someone softly whispering, "Honey! Honey!"

Half asleep, I rose up in bed and said, "What's goin' on? Who is it?"

"It's me, Sally!"

"What time is it?"

"It's after two in the morning, but I couldn't wait to see you!"

She planted a big kiss on me, and then leaned back. "You have hair on your chest!" She seemed amazed that I had hair on my chest.

"It just kinda grows on you," I said, still half asleep. I did notice that she had my neckerchief on, the one I had tied around her neck to seal our engagement the summer before.

"Not on me," she said adamantly. "Our flight was delayed for a few hours, we were late getting in."

She planted another kiss on me. "You go back to sleep," she said. "I'll see you in the morning." She left and went to the lodge.

I went back to sleep, not sure if I knew that what had happened was a dream or for real.

The next morning, Pat and I gathered the saddle horses then went to the lodge for breakfast. We were the first ones in and shortly Bud came into the kitchen.

"Good morning!" Bud yawned a little as he made his greeting. "It's good to be on the home place!"

As we greeted Bud, I got the feeling that he didn't really like to leave the ranch. Pat filled Bud in on what we'd got done while he was away.

"That's good," said Bud. "Did you graduate, Honey?"

"Certainly," I said. "Was there any doubt?" I made the last comment, knowing there was some doubt in my mind if I would graduate on time.

"That's good. We'll discuss your plans later. Right now, I think we'll run in the broodmare bunch, look over the colts and brand them. We'll need to take pictures for registration purposes. Then we'll run in the yearlings and two year olds. We can start messing with the two year olds. We've got plenty to do with them. We also need to figure out when to have our first dispersal sale. We're getting too many horses around here. And we've got a load of cattle coming in two weeks."

"Cattle? What cattle are coming?" I hadn't given much thought to the cattle side of Bud's operation. I had been mostly interested in the horse operation and been involved extensively in the dude part. What cattle work we had done was done as a necessary part of the operation, but it had been done with the dudes. I had figured the cattle were just around to give the dudes some riding to do.

"The cattle that are coming are the replacement heifers we bought from your dad last fall, Honey," said Bud. "They've all been bred to calve thirty days before the regular cow herd, around the first of February."

Sally came in for breakfast. I rose to greet her and she planted another big kiss on me. She was not at all bashful about kissing me in front of others. I noticed she was still wearing my neckerchief.

"Here, daughter," said Bud, "sit down and eat your breakfast, not him!"

Bud's comment caused Sally to break the hold she had on me.

"You're lookin' good," I said, blushing. "It's good to see you! I didn't know if I was dreamin' or not last night."

"You weren't dreaming, Honey," said Sally.

I noticed that Missus Abercrombie had not come to breakfast, and inquired.

"She'll be down shortly. The trip was a little taxing on her," said Bud.

After breakfast, we went to the corrals to saddle horses to gather the broodmares. I saddled Drygulch, thinking that Pat might want to use me as bait again. Pat saddled his personal horse and Bud saddled his big paint. Sally wanted to use her grulla, Beauty, but Bud and Pat wouldn't let her. The grulla hadn't been used since the Christmas school break and might need a little riding beforehand.

Sally, a little disgruntled, put her saddle on another horse. Pat assured her the horse was all right, he'd rode the horse a few days ago.

I noticed Pat had replaced the lariat rope on his saddle with his bull whip.

"You figurin' on usin' me for bait again?"

"If we have to," said Pat. "We might not need to, that stud's pretty wise. The treatment we gave him last year might have been enough."

"I hope so," I said.

"I was hoping to see a little action," said Bud. "I missed it last year."

Jim and the girls set about doing the housekeeping chores.

Missus Abercrombie showed up and set about helping Jim and the girls. Jeff was instructed to clean up around the barn.

We located the broodmares and the stud came out to meet us. Pat took down the bullwhip, cracked it once, and the stud returned to the mares. Sally and Bud took the lead, and Pat and I followed, keeping a close eye on the stud.

After a time, we had the horses corralled and we took a few minutes to survey the colts, then started the fire to get the irons hot. Sally went to the lodge to get the camera.

I was selected to rope the colts, being reprimanded to "not let the colts hit the end of the rope hard!" Pat and Jeff were to hold the colts. If we had to, we could use the gate as a chute to help keep them still. Bud would apply the irons, marking the colts for life. Sally took pictures and identified the colts with their mothers for registration purposes.

The branding went well, although Pat got kicked pretty good once.

"You want to rope an' let me hold 'em?"

"Nah," said Pat. "I'll be all right."

"We can take a little break," said Bud, noticing Pat limping a little.

"What do you think of this crop of colts, Honey?" Bud asked

"They all look good to me," I said. And they did look good. There was a lot of color, although there were two colts that were solid colored. "Those two colts won't bring much at the paint horse sale," I added, pointing toward the solid-colored colts.

"No," said Bud, "but I know what to do with them."

I convinced Pat that he should do some roping and I'd help hold the colts. Having them braced up against the corral fence, they didn't move much.

Sally got pictures of each colt and of each side of the colt.

When we were done, Bud said, "Let's take these horses back to their range. On the way back, we can run in the yearlings and two year olds. It's getting a little late, but we can separate them tomorrow and start messing with the colts Honey is going to break. We'll be able to get an early start in the morning after the daily chores are done."

"We got some extra chores tonight," said Pat. "We'll lock these horses in the corral then we'll show you. We can do it horseback."

Bud and Sally took the lead, the broodmares followed, and Pat and I brought up the rear. It wasn't long before we turned the horses loose on their range. We came back another way, located the young horses and brought them to the corrals. Then we started out for the branding corrals where we'd captured the wild horses.

"Just what do you have to show me?" Bud was curious.

"Honey an' me, well, we got a surprise for you. You'll see," said Pat.

Presently we arrived at the branding corrals. The mustangs were still corralled and had cleaned up the hay we'd been feeding each day. I got off my horse, handed the reins to Sally to hold while I threw out some more hay and turned on the water.

"How did you get these 'rangs in here?"

"I led 'em an' Honey brought 'em," said Pat. "We roped the two studs, cut 'em an' we're tryin' to guess what you will do with 'em."

"That's not hard to figure," said Bud. "They ain't worth much and the quality just isn't there, even though they're all young horses, two, maybe three years old. You can take them to the sale. You and Honey can split whatever they bring; I'm not interested in them.

"I was wondering where you parked your truck, Honey. It's way too far from the ranch out here. When Pat takes the broom-tails to the sale, come out here and bring your truck back to the ranch. You can park it behind the barn. It'll be close enough where you can get it if you need it."

"I figured you'd send them to the sale," said Pat. "There's enough hay in Honey's truck to keep 'em tonight, then I'll run 'em to the sale tomorrow."

"You know we have dudes, ah, that is, guests arriving tomorrow," said Bud.

"Yep," answered Pat. "I can hang around long enough to help get the horses assigned, then come and load the horses. Honey and Sally can handle the first rides. I just need to drop the horses in the sale pens, they can mail a check. I'll be back in time for supper."

The ride back to the ranch was leisurely, with Sally and me following side by side. Our conversation rambled all over, with Sally always directing the conversation back to how glad she was that I was here. Occasionally, she would lean over and kiss me. I was at a loss as to what to do or say, so I just rode along enjoying the company and the activities.

That night after supper and some general instructions as to how we were to act around the guests, Sally took my hand and led me down to the barn. I knew we were going to have some more kissing practice.

The practice session started out with Sally saying, "I love you Honey! I'm sure glad you're back!"

Then she gave me a big, long kiss. When she finally stopped for a breather and loosened her hold on me, I took a long breath and said, "Well, I'm glad to be here an' I'm glad you're glad." Reaching for my pocket, I continued, "I, ah … I have …"

I stopped cold. The ring and the little case it was in was gone! Panic set in! *I lost it,* I thought. *Where could I have lost it?* In my mind, I retraced my steps from the airport to the ranch and replayed everything I'd done since I'd got here.

"Well, what?" Sally sounded somewhat impatient.

Still feeling in a state of panic, and trying to figure out where I had lost the ring, I said, "Well, I need to show you just how much I appreciate me bein' here!"

With that, I pulled Sally close and gave her a kiss. The move surprised Sally a little; she wasn't used to me taking the initiative. The move surprised me also, I wasn't used to taking the initiative either! But as I did this, I was trying to figure out where I had lost the ring.

My mind stopped at my truck. I had put the ring in the jockey box of the truck! I remembered now. I couldn't give Sally the ring until I had it and I wouldn't have it until I had my truck. My state of panic settled into a state of relief.

The next day after breakfast we separated the yearlings and two year olds and took the yearlings back to their pasture. The two year olds would be kept with the saddle horses and brought in every day. I could start riding them after we did some groundwork and saw how well they remembered their halter breaking lessons.

Right before the noon meal, the first guests arrived. We greeted them, made introductions all around, helped get their luggage into their cabins, and went to eat. I did get some strange looks when I was introduced as "Honey," but I was getting used to it, even though I blushed a little every time I heard it. The guests didn't feel much like riding right off the start as they'd put in a long morning driving to the ranch.

We started catching the two year olds, haltering them, and tying them to the corral. Pat had halter broke them when they were weaned, and they were being handled now for the first time since then. A little time tied to the corral and being brushed would do them some good.

"You need to be thinking of names for these colts as you're breaking them," said Sally. "They've all been registered as 'unnamed.' Pick suitable names for their registration papers."

I dodged the hooves of one of the colts as he tried to kick me. "How's about Knothead?" I had some other ideas, but decided not to voice them.

The afternoon went well, just playing with the colts. A few of the dudes wandered down to the corral just to see what we were doing with the horses. I answered questions from the dudes about halter breaking the colts, and questions about horses in general. But when I was asked. "How did you come by the name Honey?" I simply pointed to Sally.

"Ask her," I'd reply.

Sally delighted in telling everyone how she'd called me Honey in front of the hired help and the nickname stuck. She would finish her story with the question, "Doesn't it fit him perfectly?"

I think she really enjoyed watching me blush.

The next day, horses were selected for the dudes and Sally and I took them out for a ride. Sally wanted to ride her grulla, Beauty, but Bud wouldn't allow it. I saddled my horse, Roman.

"We don't have time this morning. We'll mess with him this afternoon, daughter."

I didn't know exactly where to take the dudes on their first ride and decided to go to the branding corrals, just to see if Pat had got the wild horses loaded and got away all right. It was a slow, walking ride and Sally rode alongside visiting with each guest.

Before we arrived at the corrals, I noticed some dust around the corrals. I motioned for Sally to come up and lead the ride so I could get to the corrals and see what was happening. Pat might be having some trouble.

Pat was having some problems getting the wild horses loaded. The two freshly cut geldings were interested in fighting and some of the horses would go up the loading ramp onto the truck, only to turn around and come back. I opened the gate and entered the corral without Pat seeing me.

Pat was red-faced, sweating, and pretty mad at not being able to get the horses loaded. We let the horses settle down some, then Pat, and me on Roman, got the horses bunched and headed them toward the loading chute. We rushed the horses and got them all in the truck. Roman and I waited in the loading chute, blocking the escape of the horses, while Pat secured the end gate on the truck.

"I'll be a little late for supper tonight," said Pat, as he caught his breath. He muttered some cuss words at the wild horses as he rested.

"Careful," I said, "the dudes are coming. We wouldn't want them to hear some discouraging words, would we?"

Pat shot me a dirty look that quickly changed to laughter as he saw me grinning at him. He must have realized how silly he looked.

Sally and the dudes were approaching.

"I'd better be going," said Pat. "I'll be plenty late as it is an' I don't want to spend a lot of time answerin' questions from the dudes. I appreciate your help Honey."

Pat got into the truck and drove off. I opened the gate and rode Roman out, closing the gate behind me.

One of the dudes watched as Roman and I rode through the gate. "How did you do that?"

"What?" Opening a gate horseback was second nature to me and I didn't think there was anything special about it.

"Opening and closing a gate without getting off your horse," answered the dude.

"It's pretty simple," I said, "it's just a matter of trainin' the horse."

"What it boils down to is that he's too much a cowboy to get off his horse," interjected Sally.

The dude said, "You mean he's lazy?"

"Not lazy! I'm just conserving energy," I said.

When we started out, I motioned for Sally to come up front. She appeared to be more than willing to ride with me.

As she approached, I said, "When we get done with these dudes, that is, ah … guests, and today's chores, I need to come up here an' get my truck. Do you want to come?"

"Do I want to come? Are you silly? Why, of course," said Sally. "Are you asking me out?"

"I guess … ah … well, yes," I said. I had asked her if she wanted to get my truck with me, and I was starting to blush.

"You've finally asked me out. This will be our first date out in the sagebrush! Isn't it wonderful? Of course I want to come," she said.

"This ain't exactly our first date," I said. "I did ask you if you wanted something to eat when I picked you up at the airport at Thanksgiving."

"True," said Sally. "But it's the first time you've specifically asked me to go anywhere with you."

"Whatever," I said. "Just leave your horse saddled an' we'll come out when we're done tonight."

"Okay, Honey."

Sally left to rejoin the tourists, but she left with a big smile on her face. I didn't know if she was teasing me or not about the first date stuff. I really believed she liked to make me and watch me blush.

We got back to the ranch, took care of the dudes and their horses, and did the evening chores. We still had time before supper to go get the truck, so Sally told Bud where we were going and what we were going to do.

"Don't be late for supper," Bud said as we left. We got on our horses and left for the branding corrals.

The ride out was pleasant. Sally and I made some small talk. When we got to the corrals, I backed the truck up to the loading chute and we loaded the horses.

I went to the passenger side of the truck and opened the door. Sally was on the driver's side.

"I'm getting in on this side," she said, "so I can sit close to you!"

"I just needed to get some stuff from the jockey box," I said, as I got the ring and put it in my pocket. I walked around to the driver's side and met Sally waiting for me to unlock the door.

"I got a … ah … little surprise for you," I said. I was already beginning to stammer and stutter. "I kinda thought, ah … well … I was sorta thinkin' you might, ah … do you think …?"

"What is it?"

"Here," I said, giving the ring box to her. I could feel my face becoming flushed. "This is for you."

Sally's eyes opened up wide as she took the box and opened it up. "It's beautiful," she cried. She took the ring and put it on her finger. "And it fits perfectly! Thank you, thank you! How did you know my size?"

She didn't give me a chance to answer. She put her arms around me and gave me a big kiss.

When she got done kissing me, which I readily accepted, I said, "I kinda thought, ah … well, this might make it a little, ah … a little more official. And you won't have to wear my neckerchief. I notice you still got it on. I had some help pickin' it out, an' we sorta guessed at the size. If you don't like it, or it don't fit right, we can take it back."

"Oh, no, Honey! It's perfect!"

Sally gave me another kiss and got in the truck. I got in and we started back to the ranch. Sally spent the whole time admiring her ring on the drive back. She would hold her hand out, and then turn it in different directions, admiring the view from all angles. She was quite pleased, and wasn't quiet about it on the way home.

When we got to the ranch, we unloaded our horses, unsaddled them, and turned them loose. It was suppertime.

Sally wasn't at all bashful about showing off her ring to everyone—the hired help and the guests included. She would hold her hand out and allow the observers to hold her hand and inspect the ring closely.

"So you've made it official," said Missus Abercrombie. "It's about time! Congratulations Sally, and to you, Honey. I hope I'm invited to the wedding! You better make it pretty quick, I may not live long enough to make it. I'm not as young as I used to be!"

Missus Abercrombie was the only one that had congratulated me. Bud noticed this and quickly added his congratulations. "Virginia," he said, "don't be rushing these kids. They're pretty young yet and there's plenty of time. They've got their whole lives ahead of them."

"You're right, Bud," said Missus Abercrombie. "But I don't know how much of life I've got left! I certainly want to be around for the big affair."

"You will be!"

I was feeling flushed and was glad when we started eating. All the questions about "When is the big day?" and "Where is this going to happen?" I referred to Sally. I was glad when supper was over and even a little happier that Pat wasn't around to harass me about who's going to wear the pants in the family.

Big Plans for the Future

I decided to wait on the porch for Pat to return. Presently, Sally joined me and then Bud joined us.

"Let's discuss your plans for the future, Honey. Just what are your plans?"

"Well," I said, "I sorta figured on workin' here year round."

"That's good," said Bud. "That's what I was hoping for. Here's the plan for this ranch as I see it. We're not going to add any more rooms or cabins. We've got accommodations for about forty or forty-five guests here now, depending on how many kids the dudes bring with them. That's plenty.

"The replacement heifers we got from your dad should be arriving shortly. We'll turn them out with the cows. They're bred to start calving about forty-five days before the regular cow herd. We'll preg check all the cows this fall, then separate the first calvers from the cows. We should be able to tell the replacements from the older cows real easy, and the colored ear tags they're wearing will make it easier. Anything that's open, we'll take to the sale.

"I'm going to build a calving shed over behind that rise, out of sight of the lodge here. We'll build a small feedlot there and we can feed our own replacements, breed them artificially and eliminate the high cost of sending them to a feedlot. We'll put in cement feed bunks and pipe and cable fencing. We're going to put a little more emphasis on the cattle part of this operation in the future. These cows are not around here to provide entertainment for the dudes."

"I really don't have any carpentry experience," I interjected. "I don't know if I can be of any help building the shed. And I've never welded."

"That's all right," said Bud. "We've got plenty to keep you busy elsewhere. We'll contract out the construction and welding."

I was relieved to hear that I wouldn't have to be involved in the construction.

"You can ride the two-year-old colts all summer," continued Bud, "and we'll decide which ones to sell and which ones to keep. We'll hold a paint horse sale in the fall, before hunting season. There are a few mares I want to cull.

"During the hunting season, we'll take out a few hunters for elk and deer. We've done a little of that in the past and Pat's a pretty good guide. And there's no sense in letting all these rooms we've got here sit idle. We'll put some of them to good use during the fall. We'll extend our dude season as far as we can into the fall.

"During the winter, you and Pat can take care of the cattle and halter break the weaner colts. The more time you take with the colts, the better off they'll be.

"We'll calve in the spring and do our branding in shifts, like we're doing now. That gives the dudes a chance to participate. We'll separate the cows that have calved into different herds, numbering about fifty. That will make our gathering easier with the dudes. We can move each little herd into a new pasture each time we brand."

"Sounds like to me that we'll have plenty to do," I said.

"Yep," said Bud. "It might be a little rough the first year, until we get a routine established. But the routine should work itself out. And I'll be around to help when needed.

"Now, just what are your and Sally's plans?"

"You'll have to ask Sally," I said.

"Well, daughter," said Bud, "let us know just what you're planning. Neither one of us knows what's going on."

"I thought," said Sally, "we'd hold the wedding right here at the ranch. We'd do it horseback of course, and ..."

Bud interjected, "You're not going to have a church wedding?"

"No, Daddy. You can't take horses into a church! And this ranch setting is prettier than any church I've ever seen."

"Just when do you plan on doing this?"

"That sorta depends on you and Honey," said Sally. "When do you want to do it? We can't do it in June, it'll have to be April or May, after the calving and before the dudes arrive. I don't want a bunch of strangers at my wedding. I don't want to do it in the winter; it would be too cold."

"You figure out the date, but it had better be a year or two off. You're still pretty young," said Bud. "You'll have plenty of time to figure things out. Don't forget to include Missus Abercrombie in your planning. She'll be very upset if she doesn't get a chance to put her two bits worth in. Let me know what you've decided. Tell me about your honeymoon plans. Honey on a honeymoon! That's amusing."

Bud got up to leave. "Make sure you get a few things you want, Honey. Don't let her ramrod you through this," he added. "By the way, it looks like you can go to that wedding of Dave's if you want to."

I felt like I'd been ramroded into this already, but the feeling wasn't all that unpleasant. I was sorta enjoying it, even though I still blushed a lot when it was being discussed in my presence. I really wasn't too interested in going to Dave's wedding. I would try to get out of going, if I could.

The next morning, Sally, Pat, and I ran the saddle horses

in before breakfast. It was always pleasing to watch Sally ride. She knew what she was doing horseback. Of course, I enjoyed watching her all the time.

At breakfast, Sally said, "I think it's time I rode Beauty. I'm going to saddle him and ride him in the corral then take him out. Anybody want to go?"

"I'd sure like to," I said, "but we've got to take the dudes, ah … that is the guests for a ride. Then I want to start with the two year olds. I won't get on any of them for a day or two; I want to make sure they remember their halter breaking. I'd like them all to turn out as nice as the colts I started last summer. By the way, I haven't seen any of them; where are they?"

"My brother pestered me enough, so I lowered the price and he bought the two I lent him last year, and I sold one to a kid that wanted to use him for a 4-H project. The other one I sold to a girl that wanted a barrel racing prospect," said Bud. "You did a real nice job with them. I hope you do as good with this crop of colts. We'll sell some of them at our paint horse sale."

I accepted his compliment without a comment, although I was pleased. I was quite proud of the way the colts had turned out.

"You better help with the grulla," said Pat. "Jeff an' I can take care of the dudes."

"Virginia and I can help with the dudes," said Bud. "Honey, you can help with Sally, but don't take all day."

"Yes, sir," I said.

At the corral, the grulla acted like a perfect gentleman while Sally saddled him.

"Better untrack him before you get on," I said. "I still don't trust him a whole bunch. But it's a good idea to untrack every horse before you get on."

"I know," said Sally, as she walked to the round corral leading the grulla.

"Want me to get on him first?"

"No," replied Sally, "I can handle it."

"If he gives you any problems, I can help out," I said. I'd saddled Drygulch and led him into the corral. I closed the gate and got on the horse, wanting to be ready in case anything happened.

Sally got on Beauty without any problem then rode him around in the round pen. The horse moved right out.

"I think we're ready to go outside," said Sally.

Still on Drygulch, I opened the gate and Sally rode out. She asked, "Where do you want to go?"

"Let's go over by where Bud's goin' to build the calvin' shed an' feedlot," I said. "You lead the way."

We rode for about an hour then returned to the ranch. The grulla acted good the whole time, even allowing Sally to lean over and give me a kiss, horseback.

We spent the rest of the day messing with the two year olds, brushing them, saddling them, picking up their feet and just generally getting them used to being around people. I got to thinking that these colts might be fairly easy to start.

A few days later, the replacement heifers showed up and we turned them loose on the summer range.

The routine began to take shape. We'd take the dudes out for a ride in the morning, sometimes sightseeing, sometimes gathering cattle and moving them to different pastures. I'd generally ride Roman or Drygulch with the dudes. Occasionally, I'd ride another horse, often a dude horse that needed some riding. In the afternoon, I'd get the two year olds and start riding them. Sally would snub the colts as I got on, then we'd ride around in the round corral, with Sally playing out a little lead as we went.

"How do you like me leading you around?"

"I don't really think much of it," I said, although, secretly, I'd follow her just about anywhere. "This leading me business will come to an end pretty soon! These colts will soon learn to walk out by themselves."

Sally nodded her head in agreement, although she had a look on her face that seemed to say, "I'll bet!"

I did begin to wonder about Pat's comment about who's goin' to wear the pants in this family. I decided I'd have to have a serious discussion about this matter with Sally later.

We got to the point where Sally didn't need to snub the colts for me to get on, and they didn't need to be led around in the round pen before starting out. Only a couple of them offered to buck during this starting procedure. I began to ride some of the colts out in the morning with the dudes.

One day, we gathered cattle to brand. I was selected to do the roping, along with Sally. I was riding one of the two-year-old colts and figured he was ready to start roping off of. I'd had a tough morning roping; I'd missed quite a few throws simply because the colt would duck away when I threw the rope. This was not unexpected as this was the first time I had roped off this colt and he didn't know what to expect. Sally had a good morning; she hadn't missed many.

One calf that I'd missed a few times had become kinda wild after being hit along side the flanks with the rope. I decided I'd rope him by the head and get him to the fire that way.

I caught him by the head and got my dallies. But the calf ran around behind my colt, getting the rope up under the colt's tail. I couldn't get the colt turned fast enough to avoid the ensuing disaster. The colt immediately bogged his head and started to buck, with the rope in that uncomfortable position under his tail. I let the rope go and started to pull the colt's head up. But I wasn't fast enough, the colt bucked harder than I thought he could.

The calf was free and he ran off, dragging my rope. The colt continued to buck. I was using both hands on my mecate trying to pull the colt's head up and stop this foolishness. But I wasn't having much success.

The colt bucked right over the branding fire, scattering the ground crew. They made for the fence and safety.

I did hear some of the dudes yelling, "Ride him, cowboy!"

And Sally's voice came out loud and clear, "Stay with him, Honey!"

The colt was getting a little tired and so was I. I was becoming loose in the saddle and I had the thought, *It would certainly be embarrassing to get bucked off in front of these dudes.*

The colt bucked into the middle of the cow herd, and he didn't have much room to buck. He finally stopped and trotted around the corral. I let him go, thinking that if he was a little tired, he might not be so inclined to do it again.

I rode him up to the fence by the branding fire. Pat came up to us, patted the colt on the neck and said, "Good job, Honey!"

"You talkin' to me or the colt?"

"Why you, Honey, why you," answered Pat. But he continued to pat the colt on the neck, grinning.

"Are you okay?" asked Sally. "I thought for a minute you were going to lose him."

"So did I," I said. "I'm okay. Does the horse have a rope burn under his tail?"

"Nope," was the reply.

One of the dudes got the rope that the calf was dragging. "Here! I got him!"

I rode over and got the rope from the dude and dallied up.

"You want me to drag him to the fire?" Sally was still horseback.

"Nope. This colt needs some additional training," I said.

I dragged the calf to the fire, although the colt walked almost sideways all the way there. He was watching the rope closely. And I was watching him closely!

The ground crew stretched the calf out. Pat showed everyone how to hold the calf down, one man's knee on the calf's neck with the man holding the calf's front leg. Another man held the calf's hind leg with the man's leg pushing the calf's other leg forward. They had the calf as long as they didn't lose their grip. They got the calf branded.

"Tomorrow," I said, "we're goin' to saddle all these colts an' let 'em drag a rope around for a few hours. They'll get used to a rope touchin' 'em all over pretty quick. We won't put up with this monkey business any more!"

We turned the cattle out and rode back to the ranch. On the way back, Sally rode next to me and asked, "When do you think I can start riding some of these colts? I think it's about time I started doing more."

"Anytime," I said, "but I think we ought to check with your father first." The idea of Sally riding some of these colts was appealing. We could get more time on each colt thereby speeding up their learning curve, and I would have more time with Sally. "You check with Bud an' see what he says about it. I don't think he wants you to get hurt. There's a little buck in some of them yet."

A few days later, as I was saddling a two-year-old colt, Sally said, "Daddy says I can ride some of the colts with you. But you're supposed to pick them."

"Okay" I said. "Put your saddle on this one, he's been coming along pretty good. And remember, we're supposed to be teaching them how to turn and stop. Be sure to use the leg cues every time you turn."

I led a wild-colored colt to her and gave her the lead.

"I know," said Sally, "I know." She seemed a little perturbed at my reminder. I might have been guilty of giving too precise of instructions, but that was my way.

We spent a lot of time riding the colts with the dudes. Sally rode some of the colts, but managed to ride her grulla on a regular basis. The summer was progressing well. The dudes were happy, the colts were getting their work on a regular basis and Matilda was doing her duty as a leader donkey for the younger kids. At the end of each week, dudes would leave and a new batch would show up.

Disaster

One morning, Pat asked me, "When's your donkey goin' to foal?"

"Foal?" I didn't even know she was pregnant.

"Yep," said Pat. "She's been makin' a bag. She's sure to foal in a week or two. Take a look at her."

I'd been watching her every morning when we ran in the horses, but not very close. She was moving good and appeared to me to be gaining weight, so I figured everything was all right. I didn't connect the gaining weight with pregnancy.

I walked over to her and took a closer look. She was making a bag! This came as quite a surprise to me.

"What's she bred to?" asked Pat.

"I don't know," I said. "I didn't even know she was bred. It could have been one of the wild horses or donkeys around our place. I'll have to keep an eye on her, she's gettin' pretty old. I thought she was too old to breed."

For the next couple of days, I watched Matilda closely as we ran in the horses. Then one day, she wasn't with the saddle horses.

"I'd better look for Matilda," I told Pat before we started the horses toward the corrals.

"Let's take the horses home first," said Pat. "Then we can look for her after breakfast."

"I'll come and help you," said Sally.

We ran the horses in and I told Pat, "I think I'd better look for Matilda now."

"You'll miss breakfast," said Pat. "Me an' Jeff can saddle the dude horses an' handle everything. Just don't be gone all day."

I switched horses from Drygulch to one of the colts I was breaking. Sally also saddled one of the colts she was riding. I looked at her, questioningly.

"I'm going to help you," she said.

"You'll miss breakfast," I said.

"I know, but this is more important and Matilda might need a nurse!"

We rode out at a pretty good trot, knowing we had a lot of ground to cover and not much time to do it in. After about half an hour, we found Matilda. She was on her feet, grazing. Lying next to her was a spotted donkey colt.

Sally was immediately off her horse, tossing me her mecate. "Oh, he's so cute!"

I missed catching the mecate and had to catch Sally's horse. I was grateful the horse was gentle and easy to catch.

Sally was on her knees, holding the colt's head. "Isn't he cute? He's just the most adorable thing I've ever seen."

I rode up to the two, leading Sally's horse. My horse was a little spooked by the presence of the newborn paint. Matilda was only showing a passing interest in Sally and her handling of the colt. The colt was already cleaned off and I figured he'd been born about three hours ago and had already sucked.

"Let him up. Let's see how straight he is an' how big he is." I said.

Sally got up and stepped back. The colt stood up and went right to Matilda and started to nurse. He was a wild-colored colt, black and white, and he stood a little taller than I thought he should have. *Matilda must have had a difficult delivery,*

I thought. I immediately checked her out. She appeared to be all right.

"We better head back to the lodge," I said. I was disgusted with myself for not bringing Matilda's halter and lead rope along. I got off my horse and fashioned a halter from my lariat rope and started to lead Matilda back. The newborn followed Matilda closely.

"I wish I had a camera," said Sally. "That makes such a cute picture! I'll get a picture when we get to the ranch."

The sight I must have made did nothing but remind me of when I had first ridden onto the Wilson ranch, leading Matilda, then called Sally, with Sassy being led by Matilda.

My colt watched the rope pretty close. This was the colt that had bucked when the rope had gotten under his tail. I was real careful to keep the lariat lead rope away from the colt's hindquarters. He had been through a session or two of dragging a rope behind him from an empty saddle, but he wasn't a hundred percent trustful of the rope yet.

The trip back to the ranch took longer than the trip out, and I was beginning to wonder if Bud would be mad when we showed up late. We finally got to the corrals.

Pat and Jeff hadn't left with the dudes yet. They were all still at the corrals and Bud was with them. I expected a good chewing out from Bud, as we had taken longer than expected.

"I see what kept you," said Bud. "Looks like you've added a critter. Let's see what you got."

I said, "Why hasn't everybody left yet? I hope you didn't delay your departure waitin' for me."

"Actually, we did," said Bud.

I immediately became embarrassed. I wasn't here to disrupt the operation of this outfit; I was supposed to be helping out.

Bud noticed how uncomfortable I was and said, "Don't worry about it. When everyone asked where you were and Pat

103

told them that you went to look for Matilda, as she might be foaling, they all wanted to see what had happened. And here they are. What kind of a foal do you have?"

"I don't know," I said. "I didn't even know she was pregnant! I don't know when she could have got bred, unless it was by one of the wild horse or donkey studs around our place. An' I don't know what would have thrown a paint colt."

"I know," said Pat. "Last spring, we left her out one night with the stud bunch that we'd brought in when we branded the colts. Remember?"

"That's right," I said, "I remember now."

"You mean that colt is by my good paint stud?" Bud was surprised.

"That's the way it appears," I said. "But Matilda was only out there one night."

"That's all it takes," said Bud, giving me an all-knowing look.

I thought there might be a double meaning in Bud's statement, but didn't pursue it.

"Let's see now," said Bud. "That means you've stolen a very valuable stud service from me, and I don't take in outside mares ... or donkeys!"

I didn't know if Bud was serious or just joking with me, but decided to stand up and say something.

"What that really means," I said, "is that your stud has violated my donkey! An' a very valuable donkey she is! She's valuable to you as a leader for these youngsters around here, an' she won't be able to work for a few days, just havin' given birth!"

The guests that had been listening looked serious, having heard this apparent altercation between Bud and myself. I could see Pat grinning as he stood behind Bud. I thought the whole situation looked fairly comical.

"If that colt is by my very valuable paint stud, that means it's a very valuable animal. And it's not a donkey, and it's not a mule, it's a hinny."

One of the tourists asked, "What's a hinny?"

Bud turned to the tourists. "A mule is a cross between a stud donkey, or Jack, onto a female horse. A hinny is just the opposite, a stud horse crossed onto a female donkey. The offspring tends to take on the characteristics of the mother. This critter, even though Honey says his donkey is very valuable, will never be worth much. He won't be much bigger than his mom."

Pat was doing all he could to keep from laughing out loud as Bud asked, "How much do you want for him, Honey?

"I don't reckon I can sell him," I said. "He ain't even weaned yet."

The tourists were fairly busy looking at the hinny, especially the kids.

"Who wants to go for a ride? Let's put the new mother away an' go ridin'," said Pat. "We've wasted enough time here."

I got off my horse and tied him to the fence, then led Matilda and her colt to an empty corral and turned them loose. Jeff brought some hay and tossed it into the corral.

Sally went over to the kids and was telling them, "We won't be able to use Matilda today. She has to take care of her new baby. We'll be able to use her in a couple of days. We'll use another horse today. Is that okay?"

All the kids consented, except one little girl. "No," she cried, "I want to ride Matilda today!" The little girl was in tears.

Sally went to the youngster, put her arm around her and said, "It's okay. When Matilda's had some rest and is taking good care of her baby, you can be the first one to ride her. But right now, you can watch her taking care of her baby."

"What's the baby's name?" The youngster seemed to be settling down some.

"I don't know," said Sally. "Maybe we'll have a naming contest to give it a name."

"I like that," said the little girl. "I think we should name it Honey, after its owner."

"That's a good idea," said Sally.

That seemed to brighten up the youngster's spirits and Sally went to change horses. I did have to admire the way she handled the dudes—the youngsters and adults. She seemed to have the right answer for every situation.

As we rode out, Sally rode up beside me. She said, "What do you think of a naming contest for the hinny?"

"That's fine with me," I said. "However, I won't allow the critter to be named after me!" I couldn't believe I was claiming the name Honey.

I almost told Sally how I had originally named Matilda, Sally, but changed her name after meeting her. I decided against it.

"So," she said, "you like your nickname!"

"Well … ah … I'm … ah … sorta gettin' used to it," I stammered.

When we were done riding for the day, we turned the horses loose. I went to Bud and told him how sorry I was that my donkey had been bred by his stud and I really hadn't meant to disrupt the day's tourist activities.

"Don't you worry about it, Honey. That little event just put the icing on the cake for this bunch of dudes. Did you see how many pictures they took? And that hinny will be the center of attention for all the dudes that come for the rest of the summer. Why we can even use pictures of that spotted hinny for our advertisements. I wished I'd have thought of it myself!"

"But I don't think you want to advertise that your stud throws spotted hinnies," I said.

"Why not? We can advertise that the stud throws spots on anything."

"Well," I said, "seein' as there wasn't a stud fee involved an' the colt was an accident, an' you think the colt will be good advertisement, an' I ain't got no use for the colt, I'm goin' to give him to you."

"I appreciate that, Honey, but you give the colt to Sally. She'll appreciate it and she's already got a contest going on to name the critter."

That night in the barn during our kissing practice, I asked Sally how she was coming with the naming contest.

"So far, the kids haven't come up with anything special. I think we'll let the contest go for a few days. What do you think?"

"It makes no difference to me," I said. "I tried to give the colt to your dad, as I ain't got a use for him, but even though Bud says he can use him in future advertisements, he didn't want him."

She asked, "What are you going to do with him?"

"I thought I'd give him to you. You seem to do good with the kids an' usin' Matilda for a leader was your idea. You're sorta in charge of the kids program here anyways. You can halter break him, an' him bein' around Matilda during the leader sessions can do nothin' but help him. He'll get used to people pretty quick, just like Sassy did."

"Just what is Sassy doing now?"

"My sister owns the donkey, she's breakin' her to ride. She wants to ride her in the 4-H parade. What are you goin' to do with the hinny?"

"I don't know what I'll do with him," said Sally, "other than what I'm doing with Matilda. I'll accept your gift and I thank you for her. What's your entry for the naming contest?"

"I don't care," I said. "She's yours."

The next morning at breakfast, Bud asked, "How are you coming with the naming of the hinny?"

"I'm getting some suggestions," said Sally. "The best one yet is Honey."

"I object to that," I said strenuously.

"You ought to name him Einstein," said Pat.

"Why?"

"Well, Bud, Honey an' myself, we wasn't thinkin' when we left the donkey in with the stud bunch last year. Name him Einstein, an' it'll give us all somethin' to think about."

Pat's comment brought a laugh from everybody and a vote was taken right there at breakfast. The colt was named Einstein.

The summer progressed. Matilda recovered from her birthing experience, Einstein was becoming used to humans, the colts Sally and I were riding were coming along nicely and the dudes were exceptionally nice. The calves were getting branded and everyone was having a lot of fun. We were having a dance once a week with Jeff and Jim providing the music. Everything was proceeding as expected, actually better than expected.

"Are you ready to go to Dave and Marie's wedding?"

I hadn't given it any thought until Sally brought it up one day.

"I hadn't really thought about it," I said. "Besides that, I ain't got a suit."

"You better be thinking about it, we'll have to leave soon. Daddy's already given his consent for us to go for a week."

"What will this outfit do without me for a week? I'm not sure I should go," I said. Actually, I didn't really want to go. Although I was getting used to meeting the guests and mixing with them, I still felt awkward in social situations and knew I'd feel funny at a wedding with a lot of strangers around.

"The ranch will be okay for a week without you. Daddy and Pat are quite capable of operating this place. They've done it before, although never without me in the summer," said Sally. "But I think they'll be all right."

"Not without both of us! Why, that's a recipe for disaster! I better not go," I said.

"Hah!" Sally's response was such that it led me to believe she didn't believe me.

A few days later, we were gathering the horses one morning when Pat's horse, at a full gallop, stumbled and fell. Pat was thrown clear of the saddle, but he didn't sit up immediately. I saw it happen and turned my horse toward where Pat was laying. I got off my horse and looked to see what I could do. He was unconscious and from the unnatural position his right leg was in, I figured it was broken.

Sally rode up. "Is he okay?"

"No," I said. "Looks like his leg is broken. You better go to the ranch an' get Bud out here with a truck, an' tell him what's happened." I didn't have to tell her to close the gate after the horses got in the corral, she knew enough to do that. "Tell him to bring something to make a splint out of, an' hurry."

Sally rode off as fast as she could get the colt to run. Pat was coming to and it was obvious he was in pain.

"What happened?"

"Your horse fell. Knocked you out. Looks like you've busted your leg," I said. "I sent Sally for help. You just rest here 'till help arrives.

I heard some cuss words from Pat that I wasn't used to hearing. Everyone watched their language fairly close and generally it was only the dudes that cussed. But Pat was in a lot of pain and there wasn't anyone around.

Shortly, Bud, Sally, Jeff, and Jim showed up. Bud had driven the truck as fast as he could through the sagebrush. Pat was sitting up when they arrived and still cussing. He saw Sally and immediately stopped.

"You all right, Pat?"

"No," said Pat. "This leg's broke an' it don't feel too good."

Bud surveyed the situation. "I think it's broken in two places an I can't set it. We'll take you to the doc's. Good thing you put a mattress in back of the truck, Jim. It won't be too comfortable going to town, but I don't think he can ride in the front of the truck. Can you get up, Pat?"

"With some help," replied Pat.

Gingerly, Jeff and I helped Pat to his feet.

"Now," I said, trying to be funny, "Walk to the truck an' get in!'

Pat gritted his teeth and laughed. Everyone else also laughed. We helped Pat to the tailgate and he sat down on it and he slowly dragged himself to the front of the pickup bed. I could tell he was in a lot of pain. Everybody else got in the truck, and I got on my horse and gathered up Pat's horse.

"You're in charge, Honey, until I get back. Just do the regular rides. Sally and Jeff will be there to help you. I'll be back as soon as I can."

"Yes, sir!"

The pickup rumbled off and I rode the horse back to the ranch. When I got to the ranch, Bud had already left with Missus Abercrombie for the hospital, with Pat still in the back of the truck. I didn't think Pat would have an enjoyable ride to town.

Sally and Jeff saddled horses for the dude rides while I unsaddled Pat's horse. It was a somber morning ride. I really couldn't think of anything funny to say. Sally did most of the talking with the dudes. She seemed up for any occasion.

She rode up to me and said, "Just act like nothing has happened. These guests are our responsibility now. There's nothing we can do for Pat at this point, Daddy and Missus Abercrombie are doing what they can."

Sally's attitude did cause me to talk to the dudes some, but I guess I wasn't as far along with my social graces as I should have been.

Later, after the ride, I asked Sally, "How old is Pat?"

"I don't know," she replied. "I think he's almost as old as Dad."

"How old is your dad?"

"I'm not sure. In his fifties, maybe sixties, I think. I know what we'll do; we'll have Jeff and Jim play tonight and we'll throw a dance. This afternoon, we'll hold a roping clinic and do what we have to in order to entertain our guests."

"Huh?" I was confused. I was concerned with Pat's condition and Sally was talking about throwing a dance.

"Yep," said Sally, "we'll throw an impromptu dance tonight. Everybody's a little down because of what happened to Pat, so we'll throw a dance and cheer them up. That's our job. The roping clinic will help get people's minds off what happened. We need to make sure everyone's having a good time."

"What'll Bud say?"

"He can't say anything, he's not here. Besides that, there's no telling when he'll be back. He might not even make it back tonight."

We held a roping clinic that afternoon and made sure everyone participated. That seemed to cheer up the dudes some. Then, at supper, Sally announced that we were having a dance and everybody was supposed to come.

At the dance, everyone had a good time and it took their mind off what happened to Pat. We were just about ready to call it a night when Bud and Missus Abercrombie showed up.

"Well," said Bud, "a dance in honor of my return? I am honored! Come on Virginia, let's shake a leg!"

Bud grabbed Missus Abercrombie and strode out on the dance floor. As he moved around the dance floor, he assured everyone that Pat was going to be all right. He really seemed to be enjoying himself. After a few dances, he excused himself, saying, "It's been a long day and we've got a big day tomorrow. I'm going to hit the sack." With that, he left and the dudes went to their respective cabins or rooms. The dance was over.

I walked Sally to the lodge. Bud was sitting on the porch, as if he was waiting for us.

I asked, "How's Pat?"

"He's got his leg broke in two places," replied Bud. "They were talking about operating when we left. He and Virginia convinced me we should come home as I couldn't do anything anyway. I'll have to go get him in a couple of days, whenever the doctor calls. So, I came home.

"Whose idea was the dance?"

"It was mine," said Sally. "Everyone seemed a little down, so I thought I'd cheer them up. So we held a little dance."

"That was a good idea, daughter, a good idea! It worked. Better hit the sack now, we've got a big day tomorrow. I was hoping to do some more branding and the construction crews are supposed to show up and start on the calving sheds and feedlot we're building. I'll come down in the morning and help you gather the saddle horses."

"Honey and I can get them in," said Sally. "You rest!"

"Are you sure? I was gathering horses a long time before you were born, young lady!"

"We can get them," assured Sally.

"Pat will be laid up for some time," said Bud. "I don't know that I can spare you for Dave's wedding, Honey."

I was relieved. "I understand," I said. I really didn't want to go and almost said it, but kept quiet, not wanting to hurt Sally's feelings.

"I better call Marie and tell her I can't come," said Sally.

"No, daughter, you can go. Honey, Jeff, and I can handle things for a few days while you're gone. I understand you're supposed to be a bridesmaid and I don't want you to miss that. Besides, I want pictures!"

112

"But Daddy," Sally said, giving Bud a hug. "This place needs me!"

"We'll suffer for a few days without you."

Sally gave Bud a kiss, came over to me and gave me a kiss, then went to her room.

"You don't mind missing the wedding?"

"No," I said, "there's too much to be done around here to be leaving now. And I'm not really comfortable in them kinda situations."

"Better get comfortable, Honey," said Bud, laughing. "Your times a coming!"

I went to the bunkhouse and bed. Jeff was still up and I told him, "I'll wake you up in the morning; you'll need to help us gather the saddle horses."

The next couple of days went pretty regular, even with Pat absent. I did what I figured needed to be done, and did the best job I could. Jeff did a good job at the branding, taking over Pat's job of holding the calves down, although one or two of them did give him a tough time of it. Sally and I did the roping and Bud did the vaccinating, cutting, and branding. It didn't go as fast as when Pat was there, but we got it done. Some of the dudes tried to rope, but they had some difficulty catching calves.

One day, Bud got a call from the doctor saying that Pat could be released from the hospital and he could get him any time. The next day Bud told us to move some cows and where to move them and went to get Pat.

Bud came back with Pat in a cast. He'd rode back to the ranch in the back of the pickup because he couldn't bend his leg to get in the cab. He couldn't move his leg. He was on crutches, but he managed to drag himself out of the truck by himself and hobbled toward the lodge.

The cook came out and met him with a cup of coffee. "You

just sit on the porch with this coffee," said the cook. "I don't need you gettin' in the way an' botherin' me in the kitchen!"

Pat took the coffee and sat down on the porch. Sally and I rode up to the porch to say hello and welcome Pat back.

"How are you feeling? We've missed you," said Sally.

"I'm okay. Just got a little hitch in my get along. Here," said Pat, handing me an envelope. "This is your share of the money we got from sellin' those wild horses we caught. They didn't bring as much as I thought they would."

I got off my horse and took the envelope. I'd forgotten about selling the wild horses, but didn't want to admit it. "Thanks," I said, taking the envelope and putting it in my pocket. "I guess a little is better than none at all. How long are you goin' to be laid up?"

"I don't know. This is goin' to take a little longer to heal than I figured. I'll be around, an' do what I can, although I won't be able to move very good. I might get started on oilin' the saddles early this year. There ain't much else I can do, but I'll do what I can."

"Don't get in the way," said Bud as he approached us, grinning.

I hadn't seen him coming. When he got close, I asked him, "Do you think it will be good advertisin' to let him hang around with that cast on?"

"Probably not," said Bud, "but I don't know where we can hide him."

"Oh, go to blazes," said Pat. We all laughed.

"Don't let them get to you," said Sally. "They can be pretty merciless!"

"You can go with 'em," said Pat.

We all laughed and Sally and I left to take care of our horses.

"We've done pretty good without Pat," I said.

"Yes," said Sally. "But it isn't the same without him. I've always felt like if something went wrong, Pat could make it right, without a problem. And he's prevented a lot of problems in the past, especially with the dudes. It was and will continue to be a little stressful without him. I'm glad you're here!"

"I can only do what I can do," I said, feeling a little selfconscious. Pat had a lot more years of experience than I did.

"You'll have to take on a little more responsibility," she said. "We'll have to keep a closer eye on the dudes, and everything else for that matter."

"I've been tryin'," I said.

"I know, Honey, I know. But haven't you noticed?"

I asked, "Noticed what?"

"Daddy's not been riding as much this year as he has in the past, and he hardly ever ropes calves anymore when we're branding."

I hadn't noticed. "You mean he's slowing down?"

"Yes," answered Sally. "And, to me it looks like he's slowing down more than he should. I don't know what's wrong, but something is. I've talked to him and he says it's just old age. But Missus Abercrombie says it's something else. I can't get him to go to the doctor's for a checkup. I don't know what's wrong."

Sally's face had taken on a very concerned, troubled look that I wasn't used to seeing on her. I began to wonder just what was happening at the Wilson ranch.

"With Pat out of commission, an' Bud slowin' down, it looks like it's up to you an' me," I said.

"Yes," answered Sally. "We're going to have to make a difference this year."

"I'll do what I can," I said. Then, trying to be funny, I asked, "Is this goin' to be a hostile takeover?"

Sally laughed. "No, silly, but we're going to have to assume more responsibility and start making some long-range decisions on our own."

"I can do that," I said, even though I had no idea of the implications that statement held.

We turned our horses loose and went to our respective quarters to get cleaned up for supper.

The next morning, after Sally, Jeff, and I had run in the horses, Pat hobbled down to the barn and began oiling saddles. He began with his own saddle and made the comment, "It looks like this year I can get all my equipment oiled at one sitting! If you use one of them dude saddles one day, I'll oil your saddle for you."

I figured that would be a plan. The thought of having my saddle oiled for me was pleasing. It was a job I really didn't care for, but one that had to be done.

Bud took Sally to town to go back East for Dave and Marie's wedding. She would be gone about a week. She had some misgivings about leaving, but Bud convinced her it was a done deal, she had to show up.

I missed Sally while she was gone, but there was plenty to keep me busy with Pat still laid up. It was just Jeff and me gathering the saddle horses and I noticed Bud hadn't been showing up. *Maybe he was slowing down,* I thought, but didn't give it much thought as I had a lot to do.

The next day the construction crews showed up with all their equipment. There were welders, welding machines, pipe and materials for building the calving sheds. I thought, *This is going to be a pretty busy place for the next couple of weeks.*

Bud showed the crews where to put their stuff. They had come with camp trailers, and could camp right on the job site, but Bud invited them to eat with us. "I'll have the cook fix up some extra food," he said. "It'll be better than what you'll get at your trailers."

Bud had marked off the area where the calving sheds and the corrals were to be built and the feed bunks were to be poured.

He had everything marked out on a crude map, and he spent all the next day with the foreman of the construction crew going over the plans. He had given this project a lot of thought.

That night after supper he informed Pat and myself that cement trucks would be arriving in two days to pour the pad for the area where the chutes and the feed bunks would be.

"I'd be interested in seein' it," I said.

"There's nothing to see now," said Bud. "I'll show it to you when it's done. Then they'll be something to look at."

Bud took Pat with him for a doctor visit when he went to pick Sally up from the wedding. She was happy to be back, and proved it with all the kisses she showered on me.

I asked her, "How was it?"

"Very hectic," she replied. "There must have been over a hundred people there. It was very fancy and I was nervous all during the ceremony."

I couldn't imagine Sally being nervous at any social function.

"I certainly don't want anything that fancy at our wedding," she said.

I was relieved. If Sally was nervous at Marie's wedding, I couldn't imagine how I would feel. She was a lot more comfortable in social situations than I was.

"I caught the bouquet," she said. "I couldn't help it. Marie threw it right at me. They'll be coming out here tomorrow. I've given them a week here free as a wedding present. They can have a honeymoon right here!"

"What'll Bud say about that?"

"He already knows. He even suggested it," answered Sally.

Dave and Marie showed up and were given a private cabin. Dave had brought his fiddle and the band of Jeff, Dave, and Jim was reformed. That night we threw a dance.

"Do you mean I have to work for our stay here?" Dave acted as if he was upset, but I could tell he was just kidding.

"Yep," I said. "An' we'll expect you to help gather horses early in the morning."

"That's all right," he said. "That was the most fun of the whole place!"

The next few weeks went by with the regular routine. Take the dudes for a ride, gather a few cattle, do some branding, doctor a few cows for foot rot or whatever ailed them. It was a pleasing few weeks, without any incidents.

Presently, the construction crews left and Bud took the dudes and hired help to the calving sheds for an official inspection. We went out horseback. Pat didn't go as he was still healing from his broken leg.

The dudes weren't really impressed, but I was. Everything had been planned with working cattle in mind. The chutes were laid out in a circular manner, to the left. A squeeze chute was placed at the end of the chutes with a man gate at the entrance to it. This would allow a man to get behind the animal in the chute and artificially breed the animal. The chutes could also be used for pregnancy checking.

There were some small pens, which Bud referred to as sick pens, and two larger pens to hold a greater number of cattle. Water had been piped into water troughs in the center of each pen. The larger pens were made of a pipe railing on the top, with cables forming the actual fence. The smaller pens were made of pipe. There were alleyways from the end of the larger pens leading to the calving sheds.

The hay storage area was situated where it was handy to the feed bunks. I was quite impressed with the layout of the place. I could tell that the dudes weren't really impressed and Bud could see it.

"What do you think of it, Honey?"

"It looks good to me," I said. "Where did you get the plans for it?"

"Actually, it's a smaller version of the feedlot where we fed out the replacement heifers we got from your dad. I made some modifications that I thought would work better for us, like all the smaller pens under the shed. The feedlot figured about six inches of feed bunk space per animal, but I went with a foot per animal. We'll have to build a fence out from the pipe wings to keep cattle in when we're preg checking. The pens won't hold them all."

"It sure looks good to me," I said. "But it looks like it's goin' to be a two-man operation to do anything."

"That's right. But what do you think you and Pat are here for? You don't expect me to do anything, do you?"

I laughed. "You're right!"

Bud gave me a dirty look, and then laughed.

Fall

The summer passed. The tourist season was essentially over. There were fewer guests, mostly older folks whose kids had left home. There were a few young families with preschool kids. Sally and Matilda had a good time entertaining the youngsters, and Einstein made a big hit with the kids.

The cast had been taken off Pat's leg and he was riding some, although he was using a cane to help him get around. He still walked with a pronounced limp.

One day, Bud came up to Pat and me. "We've got to start planning for the fall," he said. "We've got a fall horse sale coming up. I've been working on a catalog for the sale. We've got to gather cattle, separate the cows and calves, preg check the cows, and separate the first calvers from the older cows. Then we have a few elk hunters coming. Are you up to gathering horses, Pat?"

"I think so," said Pat. "I can hang this cane on the fence while we're ridin'."

"I want to get the horses in early, so we can wean and halter break the colts. There's a few of the older mares I want to sell."

I asked, "What are you goin' to do with the two solid-colored colts you got?"

"I have special plans for them," said Bud. "But we need to

figure out what yearlings and what two year olds we want to sell and which ones we want to keep."

"How many of the two year olds do you want?" I was thinking Sally and I would make the selections as we rode the colts the next couple of days.

"They're still a little young to use in the dude string," said Pat. "They need to be a little older an' have more experience behind them before we go to putting dudes on 'em."

"They're all colored enough where they'll bring a good price," said Bud. "You and Sally figure out what ones you want to keep and we'll sell the rest. Keep two apiece and pick ones that will work into the dude string nicely in a few years. We'll have to do more riding on the ones we keep and we can do that when we're calving. There's nothing that makes a good cow horse like using them to calve out heifers.

"You and Sally will ride the colts through the sale ring. We'll sell them as started ranch colts."

"Where are you goin' to put the sale ring?" I asked. I hadn't given the sale much thought, but I could see Bud had.

"We'll rent a big tent, and have a stand brought in and make a ring out of panels I've bought. We'll make the tent right next to the big corral. We can ride the horses in the big corral as a preview area.

"The cook will set up a barbeque in a corner of the tent to feed everybody. The housekeeping staff can help the cook. We're going to charge a minimal fee for the food and rooms or cabins for those that want them. We'll also have a place where people with trailers can camp. There'll be a fee for that also. I've explained all that in the catalog."

"How come you're charging for all that?" I didn't think the Wilson ranch really needed the money that bad.

"It's explained in the catalog," said Bud. "For those folks that buy a horse, there won't be a room or camping fee. I'll deduct that from the sale price of the horse. I don't want to be furnishing a free place to stay for people that are just looking and are not planning on buying.

"I've hired the auctioneer from the sale barn to handle the details of the sale and he's bringing his staff, secretaries, and ring men out with him. I want this to run smooth, but this is our first sale so there's bound to be some glitches.

"Honey, you, Sally, Pat, and I will sort through the yearlings and figure out what ones we want to keep. I don't think we want to keep many to start breaking next year. We'll have plenty to do.

"Honey, your dad said he was interested in buying a few horses. I talked to him on the phone a few days ago. I told him you'd started all the colts and you could inform him as to which ones would work best in his operation. He's bringing the whole family, even your mother, so be on your best behavior!" Bud was grinning when he made the last comment.

I tried to be on my best behavior all the time at the Wilson ranch, but was surprised to hear Bud had been talking to my dad. I knew some of our horses were starting to get some age on them, particularly my old saddle horse, Charlie, that I had given to my brother Tommy a few years before as a Christmas gift.

I figured all the colts would work good for Dad, but started trying to figure out which ones would work the best.

Sally and I made our decisions as to which of the two year olds to keep and which ones to sell.

We gathered the broodmare bunch, and I noticed that Pat replaced his rope with the bull whip.

I asked, "Expecting some problems?"

"Not really," answered Pat. "But it's good to be prepared."

After we gathered the broodmare bunch, and separated the colts from the mares and a few older mares that Bud wanted to sell, we turned the broodmare bunch back out. The next few days were spent halter breaking the weaner colts, brushing the yearlings and riding the two-year-old colts that were going to be sold.

"Fall's a bad time to sell," said Pat, as he brushed one of the colts. "We've weaned a little early an' it's hard to brush these colts enough to make them look good with their winter coat growin'. You know a horse sheds his coat twice a year, Honey?"

"Yes," I said. "The winter coat that comes in is coarser an' grows longer."

"Most people don't know that! Sometimes you amaze me," said Pat, grinning.

"Well, I'm not as dumb as I look," I said. "And don't say 'I certainly hope not!'"

The tent company showed up and set up the tent and the auctioneer showed up with a stand and a microphone system. All sorts of electrical cords were laid out to provide electricity for lights and the sound system. The place took on a carnival-type appearance.

The cook set up his portable barbeque equipment in the corner of the tent. He told everyone that he was ready. Josie was selected to take the money and make change.

I was amazed. There was more to this event than I had figured. But Bud had taken all that into account.

My folks showed up a day early. I helped them unload their luggage into the cabin where they were going to stay. My mother's first comment was, "I really want to thank you for all the cards and letters you sent! Here's some winter clothing you might need."

To be truthful, I hadn't sent any. "I've been pretty busy," I said. I took the clothing and set it aside. I'd take it to the bunkhouse later.

"It's a good thing Sally is here. She kept me fairly well informed about what was happening. How's Pat?"

My mother gave Sally a big hug.

"Pat's coming along as well as can be expected," answered Sally. "But these things take time. He's been doing what he can and he's really been a big help to Honey."

Sally made the last comment like I had become the foreman and Pat had been regulated to a hired hand. I was surprised. Without knowing it, I had taken over Pat's duties and responsibilities. It didn't seem like to me that I was doing any more than what was required. And Pat hadn't said anything.

"Have you selected some good colts for us? You know our horses are starting to show some age," said my dad.

I started to take my dad to the horse pen when my sister Betty asked, "Where's Matilda? I want to see her."

I took Betty and showed her where Matilda was and they immediately became reacquainted. Then I took my Dad and Tommy to the pen where the two year olds were and told them a little about each colt.

"What's that one?" My dad was pointing to a paint colt that I hadn't described.

"That colt got a rope under his tail last summer and really went to buckin'. He almost bucked me off. I've been ridin' him quite a bit, but he still watches a rope pretty close. He just needs some more ridin'. He's still learnin'."

"Is Bud figuring on selling him?"

"No," I said. "I figured I'd keep him an' put some more miles on him. He should be a pretty good horse when he grows up. But it will be a long time before he becomes a horse that we can let the dudes ride. He actually handles pretty good."

"That's interesting," said Dad. "I kinda like him a little better than the rest. I'll talk to Bud about him. What can you have Tommy do during the sale?"

I couldn't believe that my dad was wanting to buy a horse that we hadn't figured on selling and that I had thought I would use as my own horse on the Wilson ranch.

"Tommy can help out by saddling a few colts before they're sold an' bringin' the saddles out of the ring. There's always brushing to do this time of year. Betty can even help out with that, if she wants to. Tommy can ride a few colts through the ring if he wants to."

I didn't know where my mother and Sally were. They'd disappeared. I found them sitting on the porch of the lodge, talking. Sally had a very serious look on her face and I decided not to interrupt them.

We got ready for supper. I told Dad, "You need to tell Bud about the success you've had feedin' the cows in the evening to facilitate calvin'. I haven't said much to him about it, an' he's really tryin' to keep up to date with the cattle part of his operation."

"I'll do that during supper."

Dad told Bud about the feeding procedures he had been using the last two years. He indicated he was pleased with the results.

"We'll give it a try," said Bud.

After supper, my dad and Bud talked and Sally and I went to the barn for our kissing session. I thought I was doing real well and looked forward to these times alone with Sally

The day of the sale arrived, along with a rainstorm. I thought it was probably snowing in the mountains. I was glad Bud had put up a big tent.

We sold the weaner colts first. Each colt was led through the ring by Sally, Tommy, or myself and Bud gave a brief description of the colt's sire and dam. The yearlings were sold next, and Bud gave a description of the sire and dam of each colt as Tommy, Sally, or me led the colts through. He had pictures of the stud, along with the bloodlines, in the catalog and posted around the inside of the tent. He told everyone that each colt had been halter broken, that all their feet could be picked up, and that they were ready to start breaking next spring. Whoever was leading the colts through picked up each foot of the colt to demonstrate how well the colt was broke and trained.

We took an hour for the noon meal after the colts were sold. I asked Bud, "How is the sale going? Are you getting enough money for each colt? Is this sale a success?"

It wasn't really any of my business, but I was interested. I didn't know if Bud was pleased or not. Apparently he was as he nodded his head approvingly, in between mouthfuls of his meal.

After lunch, we sold the older broodmares. Bud was careful to tell the buyers the reason he was selling each mare and indicated which ones had been broke to ride, although they hadn't been ridden for a while.

Next, it was time to ride the two year olds through the ring. Sally started and rode her colt into the center of the ring and put it through its paces. Bud explained that each colt had between ninety and a hundred days of riding and that it was outside riding—gathering cattle and taking the dudes out. He told everyone that all the colts had been roped off of, although he indicated that not all the throws had been successful. The crowd had a good laugh.

I was careful to remind Sally to untrack the colts she was riding through the ring. I was careful to untrack the colts I rode through the ring. I was just a little leery of getting on a cold-backed horse. However, Pat was in the background, helping Tommy brush and saddle the colts. He also untracked the colts before Sally or I got on them.

The colts were ridden into the ring. We showed everyone what they could do. Occasionally Bud would ask Sally or me a question about the colt, and we would answer as honestly and positively as we could. Then we'd unsaddle the colts so everyone could see their back, pull the hackamores, and leave the ring. We generally didn't get to hang around long enough to hear the final sale price.

Every now and then, a round of applause was heard from the buyers.

"What's goin' on?" I had never heard applause at a horse sale before.

"That indicates that the auctioneer has brought a fairly high price for the horse. I never have figured out if the applause is for the auctioneer or the person who bought the horse," answered Pat.

When the last colt was sold, Bud announced, "There'll be another sale in the future, probably two years from now, with more fine, young horses to be sold. If you want a catalog, be sure to put your name and address on our mailing list. Thank you all for coming and helping to make this sale a big success!"

It was clear that Bud was pleased with the results of the sale. We helped load the colts into trailers and trucks that the buyers had brought. Some of the colts were reluctant to get into the trailers, but we managed to coax them in.

"I'll get a horse trailer this year," said Bud. "We need to teach all our colts how to load."

After all the buyers had left with their new horses, we took a minute to relax.

"Might just as well eat supper here," said the cook. "I've got enough here to feed everyone."

I looked at my watch, it was close to suppertime.

"Sounds like a plan," said Bud.

During supper, I asked my dad, "You didn't get anything, did you?"

"Oh, yes I did," said Dad.

"What did you get?"

"I bought that colt you showed me yesterday. The one that got a rope under his tail. And I bought Pat's private colt. I paid plenty for them, but they're good horses."

"Pat's private colt! Which one is that?" I was surprised that

I had been riding Pat's colt and even more surprised that Pat would let me. Nobody had told me.

"That's the one you call Numbskull," said Pat. "He's a better horse than you thought."

"Looks like to me," I said, "that you owe me a horsebreakin' fee. I had to spend a lot of time with that colt; he's a slow learner!"

"Hah! But what he learns, he remembers," answered Pat.

"How are you goin' to get them home, Dad? You didn't bring a truck."

"I've got that figured," said Bud. "You're going to deliver them, day after tomorrow, in your truck."

I immediately thought Bud was firing me and sending me home. I must have had a surprised look on my face, because Bud said, "I'm not sending you home, you're just delivering your dad's new horses. You'll have some time to visit with your folks and relax for a day or two."

"Can I go? I could use a little relaxation," said Sally.

"Yes, daughter, you can go. You can use a little rest before we start gathering cattle and get into hunting season. On the way back, you should stop in town and get Honey some winter clothing. It can get pretty cold up here in the winter."

I'd looked through what Mother had brought me and thought I had enough. I didn't know what Sally had for winter clothing.

My folks spent the night at the Wilson ranch and left the next day. Before they left, my dad admonished me, "You drive careful with my new horses. I paid plenty for them!"

"Yes, sir!"

The next day, Bud had me catch up the two solid-colored colts he didn't sell. I asked Bud, "What do you have planned for these colts?"

"You'll see."

Presently a truck and trailer pulled into the ranch. A man

and two kids, about ten or twelve years old, got out. The man walked up to Bud and shook hands.

"You sure you want to do this?" the man asked.

"Absolutely," said Bud. "Already got it figured. Here are the transfer papers, the brand inspection, everything you need. We'll help you get them loaded."

"What's goin' on?" I asked Pat.

"Bud promised those kids a couple of horses awhile back for 4-H projects," answered Pat. "Those solid-colored colts wouldn't have brought much at the sale, although they can be registered as breeding stock only, sort of an appendix registry. But they'll fill the bill for those kids' projects."

We got the colts loaded and the family left.

"Better get your truck and get going," said Bud. "When you get back, we'll start our fall gather."

I went to where I'd parked my truck and started it. I had been careful to run it once a week, just to keep the battery charged up. As I drove the truck up to the lodge, Bud met me.

"Fill your tank at our gas tank," he said.

I was grateful for Bud's invitation. I wasn't sure I could make it to town with the gas I had in the tank.

"Make sure you fill it before you come home and get a receipt. I'll reimburse you for it. And get a receipt for your meals, I'll pay you for them, too," he added.

Sally brought a suitcase and we loaded the horses and set out for my dad's ranch. We stopped for something to eat in town and decided to do our shopping on the way home.

My dad met us at the loading chute when we arrived at the ranch. We unloaded the horses and Dad gave them each a measure of grain.

"I'll keep them in for a few days, grain them every day so they learn where their new home is, then turn them out with the other horses."

We went to the house and my mother's greeting to Sally indicated more than just a passing friendship. I was glad to see they were getting along so well. I had it figured that my mom was going to be the mother that Sally never knew, although Missus Abercrombie seemed to fill the roll quite well. We had supper and afterward Dad and I talked the cattle business, range conditions and the like while Mother and Sally did the dishes and discussed our upcoming wedding.

Sally asked, "Didn't this used to be your job, Honey?"

"For a while," I replied. "But I graduated, remember?"

The next day, we all went for a ride to look at the country. We didn't really have anything to do, but it was a nice way to spend the day. Dad rode his new horse and Tommy rode the other one. I rode one of Dad's horses as did Sally. Mother rode one of the ranch horses and Betty rode Tommy's horse, Charlie.

Dad was pleased with the way his new horse handled and Tommy got along good with Numbskull. *That's a good match*, I thought. Probably some brotherly competition coming into play.

We spent a good day visiting. Mother and Sally spent a lot of time talking and I didn't know exactly what it was about.

Dad and I spent a lot of time discussing Bud's operation. Dad had seen the calving shed and feedlot and was impressed.

"Cattle, horses, dudes, and some hunting. That's a lot of responsibility you're marrying into. You'll be pretty busy year round. Are you up to it?"

"I think so," I said. "We'll find out soon enough."

"When are you figuring on tying the knot?"

"I don't know," I said. "You'll have to ask Sally."

"Seems like to me," said Dad, "that you don't know much to be marrying into that family and assuming a lot of responsibility. I suspect that your mother probably knows more about it than you do." He was halfway laughing when he said that.

"I'll bet she does," I said. "Her and Sally have been doin' a lot of talkin' while we've been here an' earlier at the horse sale. I'll bet they got it all figured out."

"I'm thinking that might be the case," said Dad.

"Well, I wish they'd tell me. Not knowin' anything has Pat believin' that Sally will wear the pants in our family."

"You just remember that marriage is supposed to be a fifty-fifty deal, but you both have to contribute more than fifty to make it work. It don't make much difference who wears the pants in the family as long as the major decisions are made with equal consideration for all concerned. It's supposed to be a democratic situation, but doesn't always work out that way. That's why a lot of marriages fail, folks tend to forget that and seem bent on being the boss, or in control of everything. You remember that, and you'll get along all right.

"Also remember that whatever you do, even if it's wrong, if it's done for the right reasons, it will be okay. But if you do something for the wrong reasons, even if it's right, it will be wrong. Keep that in mind always."

I was a little confused about that and decided that I'd have to give Dad's statement a little more thought.

The next day we left for the Wilson ranch. We stopped to do some shopping in the larger town. I didn't think I needed anything, but did buy a bigger coat and a couple of extra pairs of long johns.

Sally was still shopping when I'd completed my purchases. I found her in the women's department, looking at long johns.

She held up a pair of long johns. "What do you think of these?"

"Are you goin' to model them?" I was only joking.

"Only if you want me to," she replied. She was grinning and I was starting to blush.

"Well ... I, ah ..." she was making me stammer and stutter. "I don't ... ah, is that a good idea?"

"I need to make sure they fit," she said.

"You go try 'em on," I said. "I'll be around here somewhere. But remember, we have to be headin' out before too long. We want to get home by suppertime, an' we still have to get somethin' to eat here."

Sally looked a little surprised at my assertiveness, but retreated to a dressing room to see if the long johns fit.

When she was through, we made her purchases, went to a café, ate, and headed home. One the way, I asked her, "What did you and Mother talk about?"

"Mostly about the wedding. I think I have everything planned, subject to Missus Abercrombie's approval and Daddy's of course. But the major details are worked out."

"You're not planning on a big wedding are you?"

"No, I don't want a big wedding. But everyone likes the idea of doing it horseback."

"That's, good," I said. "It will be hard for my knees to be knockin' if I'm horseback."

Sally laughed. "When do you want to do it?"

"I don't know," I said. "Whenever you want. We need to make sure that we have time between the calvin' an' the arrival of the dudes."

"How does the first part of May sound to you?"

"That's good," I said. "What year?"

"Why, next year of course!" Sally was laughing. "Do you think that's rushing it?"

"No. What does my mother think of it? And what does your dad think of it?"

"Your mother's in favor of it," replied Sally, "if we're both set on it. She said she'd talk to your dad. I don't know what Daddy thinks of it. I'll have to talk to him."

Sally informed me that my mother had volunteered her wedding dress for her, but she declined, saying that Betty would probably want it, and she thought her dad still had her mom's wedding dress.

She asked me, "What are you going to wear?"

"I don't know. I'll probably get a new pair of Levis and a new shirt. Perhaps a new hat. Maybe even a tie. They wear ties at weddings, don't they?"

Sally laughed and slapped me on the shoulder. "Of course, silly. But this is a formal affair; you'll need to rent a tuxedo."

"A tux?"

"Yes. I'm not marrying some range rider that just drifted in for a free meal and a place to spend the night."

"But that's about the way it happened," I said.

"True," said Sally. "But you are just you, not trying to be something you aren't. And, I saw some things in you that I liked. Things that maybe you weren't even aware of and still possibly might not even know. But that's all right, I like what I see and I really love you!"

I was starting to blush again. "I don't know what it was, but you're stuck now. You talk to Bud and whatever you decide is okay with me. Don't forget to consult with Missus Abercrombie."

"Fine. You leave all the hard jobs to me!"

I laughed and we continued to the ranch. When we arrived, I noticed a new horse trailer in the yard. He'd gone to town and bought one. Bud was serious when he said that we'd teach the colts how to load in a trailer.

The next day, Sally and I ran the saddle horses in. The rest of the hired help had left, as the tourist season was pretty well over. It was just Sally, Bud, Pat, the cook, myself, and Missus Abercrombie left at the ranch. There would be some hunters showing up later, and Bud wanted to get all the cattle gathered before hunting season.

The cook stayed at the ranch while the rest of us set out to gather cattle. We all picked mature horses to ride on our first day of gathering. I rode Drygulch; Pat rode his own horse, the one that had stumbled with him and he'd ended up with a broken leg. Bud rode his big paint, and Sally rode her grulla. Missus Abercrombie rode the dude horse she'd been riding all summer.

It was kinda different, riding without any guests and not having to keep an eye on anyone. We got quite a ways out on the summer range when Bud stopped.

"Sally, you and Honey ride north to the fence and bring everything here. Pat, Virginia, and I will ride west and we'll meet you here with whatever cattle we get. If you get here before us, make sure you wait for us. Don't start home until we meet you. We'll turn these cattle loose and come out tomorrow and ride the other half of this range. It'll take more than two days of riding to gather everything. Remember to bring the cattle slow so the calves stay with the cows. A lot of the calves are already weaned, but they'll travel better with their mothers and we won't have so much trouble."

Sally and I headed out. I remarked to Sally, "It looks like Bud has given us the big circle to gather."

"That's what I expected," said Sally. "But look at how old they all are, and Pat, even though he's somewhat younger than Daddy, isn't completely healed yet. He's still favoring that leg some."

"True, true, Darlin'. But we can handle it, can't we!"

"You bet! I'll even bet you that I can gather more cattle than you can!"

"You're on," I said.

When we came to the fence, we split up and started pushing cattle back to where we had left the other three riders. Sally went to the east where she could use the fence to help push the cattle toward the appointed meeting place. I found a few cows close and pushed them toward where Sally was working.

I found more cattle and being a considerable distance from where Sally was working, started them toward home. I spotted some cattle a ways from where I was working. I rode over to them and pushed them toward my main herd then continued to move them toward home.

I lost track of Sally, but could see she had a big bunch of cattle gathered from the dust they were stirring up. I had a considerable herd gathered, and was adding to it every mile. Eventually, the cattle Sally had gathered and the herd I gathered merged. We had a big herd and I was glad we had a fence on one side to help us keep the cattle headed in the right direction.

I rode out on the flank and Sally rode drag. When we got to the spot where we were supposed to meet the others, they were waiting for us. They had some cattle gathered. We had a sizeable herd gathered. We let the cattle rest for a while and Bud told us that he'd count them as we filed them into the holding pasture close to the ranch. Then he looked at Sally.

"My goodness, daughter, didn't you wash your face this morning?"

Sally was covered with dust. "Of course I did," she said, smiling. "But I've gathered more cattle than anybody and done more work than everybody. I have earned the right to be dirtier than anybody." With that, she wiped her sleeve over her face, removing a lot of the dust.

"Don't you forget, Darlin', that I pushed a lot of them cows toward you," I said.

"Only so as I'd get dirtier," she replied.

Everyone had a good laugh and we started the cattle toward the ranch. Bud rode at the point, Missus Abercrombie rode swing, and Pat was on the flank. Sally and I rode drag, the dirtiest position. Missus Abercrombie was having some trouble keeping her section of the herd in line and Pat waved to one of us to take over his position while he went to help her.

"You go," I said. "You're already dirty enough. I'll handle this here."

Sally left and we continued moving the cattle toward the ranch. When we got to the holding pasture, Bud threw open the gate, moved back a little and started counting the cows as they went through the gate.

When we had all the cattle in the holding pasture and closed the gate, Bud said, "That's about half of them. Tomorrow we'll get fresh horses and see how many more we can find. It'll be a rougher ride tomorrow. The country we didn't cover is rougher, and harder to gather. How are you holding up, Virginia?"

"I'm okay," she replied. "I'm actually a pretty tough old bird, even though some of those cows wanted to try me. It's a good thing Pat came up and gave me a hand, I was having my hands full and my poor horse was getting tired."

"We couldn't have done it without you," said Bud, "we appreciate your help. And you, daughter, make sure you clean your face good before supper. You look like you've been dragged through the horse corrals!"

"My face! That's not all I'm going to clean," said Sally. "The way I feel, I think I'll get in the shower and go for an all over cleaning."

"Make sure you grain your horses good before you do any personal cleaning," said Pat. "Even though we're all dirty, the horses are the ones that have done all the work. They deserve a good reward."

"That's right," added Bud. "But I'm pleased with what we have accomplished so far. We've put in a pretty good day."

When we got to the barn, we unsaddled, grained the horses, and turned them loose. I was surprised that Missus Abercrombie even unsaddled her own horse, a chore that she had left to the hands, along with the other dudes, all summer.

"You've become quite a hand," I told her, as she carried her saddle to its rack.

"I could have done this all summer long," she said. "I just

didn't want to set a bad example for the other dudes. I know how particular you are about everything being put in its proper place."

"Oh, that's Pat," I said. "I ain't that fussy."

"Oh, yes you are! I've watched you the last couple of years. You're both cut out of the same mold!"

That came as a compliment to me. I had a lot of respect for Pat, as he was a good hand. He knew cattle and horses and was an excellent horseman.

That night at supper, everyone came to eat cleaned up as best as they could. Sally and I went to the barn to practice kissing after supper. Our practice session didn't last long, as we were both tired and we both knew we had a big day ahead of us tomorrow.

The next day, I saddled Roman and everyone else saddled the dude horses they wanted to ride. We rode to the summer pasture and again split up to gather cattle. Again, Sally and I got the big circle.

Before we split up, Sally asked, "Do you want to wager on who brings in more cattle?"

"Nope," I said.

"How come?"

"Yesterday you counted the cattle I brought to you as yours," I said. "A feller ain't got a chance that way."

Sally laughed. "I didn't think you'd catch on that quick," she said. She continued to laugh as we split and started hunting for cattle. And she was still laughing as I pushed cattle toward her and she pushed them along the fence toward our meeting place.

Once again, we met Bud at the appointed place and started the cattle toward the holding pasture. None of us were as dirty as we were the day before, but we were all tired.

Bud counted the cattle as they entered the holding pasture. After we had pushed the cattle in and closed the gate, Bud said, "If my count's right, we're missing about twenty-six head, along with their calves. We'll sort the calves off tomorrow and put them in our new feedlot to wean them. There's hay over there and we can start using the pens right away. Then, the day after that, we'll ride for the missing cattle. It'll be tough, but we want to get all the cattle we can before the vet arrives to preg check next week. I don't want to winter anything over that's not going to calve."

The next day, Sally and I each saddled one of the two-year-old colts I'd started the previous spring. Everyone else saddled a dude horse. This was going to be a fairly easy day, separating the cows from the calves. But there would have been a lot of footwork if we hadn't saddled the horses.

We separated the cows and calves, put the calves in the new feedlot, and trailed the cows to another pasture where they wouldn't get mixed with any other cattle we found.

The following day, we saddled the horses we'd used on the first day of the gather and started out to hunt for the missing cattle. We expected to cover the whole area, what we had taken two days to ride, in one day. We left the ranch at a brisk trot, figuring saving some time. Missus Abercrombie didn't accompany us.

"It'll be too tough a day for her," explained Bud. "She's starting to show her age and the last couple of days have taken their toll on her."

When we got to the summer pasture, we stopped to let the horses blow. Bud explained, "We'll ride this again. Bring everything you see. Also, let me know if you come across any dead carcasses. We need to account for everything we turned out during the summer."

We separated and this time Sally and I separated earlier than we had a few days before. This was it. We had to find everything or the missing cattle might stand the chance of starving to death during the upcoming winter. For them, it was a matter of life or death.

I found a few cows and when I met up with Sally, she'd found a few also. All together we had eleven pairs.

"You take these cattle toward the meeting place," I told Sally. "I've got another area to ride. I'll meet you there."

Sally didn't object. "Be careful, Honey," she said, as she started the cattle.

I had an area to ride that I'd just looked at previously. I hadn't spotted any cattle there and had my hands full with the cattle I already had. I headed out at a fast trot.

Along the way, I spotted the carcass of a dead cow. *There's one already accounted for,* I thought. I headed out a little faster, hoping to find live cattle.

I topped a rise and spotted three cows and their calves below me. I started the cattle toward the meeting place at a trot and went beyond them to look for more cattle. I did find another cow and calf, and took them toward the three pairs I had already found.

I'd found only four pair and one carcass. I hoped the others had more luck than I'd had. Between Sally and me, we had fifteen pairs and one carcass. That made ten pairs and one leppy calf that were still missing.

When I caught up to Sally, she was already in sight of Bud and Pat. They were too far away to see how many pairs they had, but from a distance it looked like they pretty well had the missing cattle.

When we reached them, Bud made a count and said, "We found six pairs and one leppy calf."

"I found the leppy's mom," I said. "She's dead over behind that far rise."

"Let's see," said Bud. "We found six pairs; you found fifteen pairs; that makes twenty-one. The dead cow makes twenty-two. That makes four pairs we're still missing. We won't worry too much about them, we can try to spot them while we're hunting."

We started the cattle toward the holding pasture, pushing them a little faster than we should have, but it was getting close to being dark. We were in a little bit of a rush and Pat was the only one that noticed the sunset and made a remark about it.

"That's almost a glorious sunset," he said.

"Why Pat," I said, "I never realized you were such a philosopher. I'm amazed."

"It is beautiful," said Sally, not slowing down. We put the pairs in a smaller pen at the calving shed, threw them some hay and went to the barn to take care of our horses. It had been a long day and all our horses showed signs of being used hard. The hands also showed the same signs.

At supper, Bud told us, "That's about the most successful gather we've ever had. We're only missing four pairs, and I'm sure we can find them during the hunting season. But we've got most all of them and I'll call the vet to see when he can come out and preg check the cows. I hope he can come before hunting season. That would make it easier on all of us."

"I thought you said the vet was coming next week," I said.

"That's true. But we're done a little earlier than I figured and next week was only tentative on the part of the vet. I need to firm him up on the deal.

"I'll also have to call some cattle buyers and have them come look at the calves, but we'll have to cut out some replacement heifers first. We'll cut the replacement heifers out first and separate them. We'll only show the other calves to the buyers. We'll need about thirty head of replacements. We can turn the cows out on the winter range after we've preg checked. We'll keep the open cows in and fatten them up a little, then take them to the sale if we can't interest any of the cattle buyers in them. Hopefully, we can sell everything and move them out within a couple of days. Then we can all take a couple of days and enjoy some hunting. Got your license, Honey?"

"Nope," I replied.

"Better get one. Sally's already got one."

"I don't know when I can get to town to get one," I said.

"If we get time, we'll manage that," said Bud.

Bud got on the phone to the vet then called some cattle buyers. The vet was coming in two days, the cattle buyers in five. The vet was going to stay at the ranch in one of the cabins and the cattle buyers were each allotted a cabin to stay in. Bud thought it would easier than having everyone come out on a daily basis. He was mighty easy when it came to providing a place for people to stay, if they had business at the ranch.

"We have the facilities, why not use them and make it easier on everyone concerned?" He was very open about it. "It will save everyone a couple of hours of travel time every day. And," he added, slyly, "it will give everyone a good feeling about this place. It will be easier to get them out here next time."

In my opinion, Bud knew how to work people to get what he wanted. The trouble was that Sally knew how to work Bud to get what she wanted. I didn't know which one was the better statesman. I thought either one would do good in politics.

The next day, we separated the pairs we had found out on the third day of gathering. We made ready for the vet to preg check the cattle. We'd cut the bulls into a separate pen as we separated the cows and calves the previous days. We took the bulls to the bull pasture, except for some older bulls Bud wanted to replace. He'd try to sell them to the cattle buyers when they were here.

"I'll go to a bull sale or two this winter," said Bud.

Hunting Season

The following day, the vet showed up and we started preg checking the cows. The vet was impressed with the calving sheds and the layout of the corrals. He particularly liked the breeding chute. It could also be used as a preg checking chute.

When we started preg checking, I was assigned the job of catching the cattle in the squeeze chute.

"That's appropriate," said Pat. "You've caught a lot of the calves this past summer. You should be pretty good at it!"

Everyone laughed, and we got started. Pat kept the cattle moving in the chute as needed. Sally operated the entry gate for the vet to get into and out of the chute and do the preg checking. Bud operated the gate that we used to separate the first calvers from the older cows. I recognized the first calvers by their ear tags; I'd put a lot of them in those ears myself. These were the replacement heifers Bud had bought from my dad the year before. They were now pregnant yearlings and we figured them to calve in the spring.

Bud also had the job of separating the open cattle from the pregnant cows. This wasn't too difficult, the gate was right across the alley from the gate where the first calvers went.

As the vet preg checked each cow, he put a number on each pregnant cow. This number indicated the number of months the cow was along in her pregnancy. Later on, we'd separate the cattle by their numbers so we could brand the calves at intermittent periods during the summer, when different groups of tourists would get an opportunity to brand.

The preg checking went on without a break until noon, when we went to the lodge to eat.

"How's everyone holding up?" Bud was always concerned with the welfare of everyone.

With an affirmative answer from everyone, we ate and went back to the calving shed to resume the procedure.

I hadn't missed a cow all morning, but was a little slow with one cow and she muscled her way through the chute. Bud cut her into the open pen, saying, "If she doesn't want to conform to our methods of doing things, she can go down the road!"

The procedure went well and the vet indicated he was getting a little tired. We figured how many more cows needed testing, and decided to call it a day. We'd checked just over a hundred cows.

"Two more days and we'll be done," said Bud. "That's good, the cattle buyers are coming the day we're supposed to be done, and we can sell the calves shortly. I'm looking forward to relaxing and doing some elk hunting. We might even have some time for Honey to go to town and get his license."

We preg checked the next two days and continued into the morning of the third. The cattle buyers started showing up and Bud invited them to look over the calves while we were finishing up. The vet made preparation to leave, saying, "I'll send you the bill."

Bud asked him, "How are you doing with your colt?"

I thought the vet looked familiar, but didn't place him with the colt buyers at the horse sale.

"The colt is coming along fine. Whoever started him did a good job."

"That was Honey here. I think Sally did some riding on him also."

"Well, you tell them they did a real good job. I'm very pleased, although this time of year, with all the preg checking going on, I don't have a chance to ride him much. But I'm very happy with the horse."

The vet left and Bud turned his attention toward the cattle buyers. "When you guys are ready, I'll show you to your cabins."

Pat was already mingling with them. He knew most of them and was having a good time visiting with them as he hobbled around with his cane. He was already explaining that we had some bulls and some open cows to sell, if they were interested. Some of the buyers took some interest in the older cattle, but most of the interest was in the calves. They were going to go to a feedlot, fattened up over the winter then be slaughtered for beef.

The cook had supper ready and everyone went to the lodge to eat. The cattle buyers were a jovial bunch, and they all knew each other from the various sales they attended.

The next morning, each buyer entered the pen with Bud and they discussed the merits of each bunch of cattle. One buyer wanted to buy the whole bunch, with the right to cut back up to ten percent for whatever reason.

Bud talked with each buyer as they made their bids. Bud finally settled on one bid for the whole bunch, minus the leppy calf. Then Bud started to talk about the open cows. Some of the buyers left, having interest only in the calves. Bud thanked them for coming, then started to talk about the cows. He entered the cow pen with each buyer and followed the same procedure with the cows that he had done with the calves. A buyer was selected, and Bud moved onto the bulls.

Soon the calves, cows, and bulls were sold. The various buyers would have their trucks here in the next few days. It looked like we'd have some free time to relax before hunting season.

I thought I'd spend some time looking for the cattle we'd missed when we gathered. We were still missing four pairs.

After supper, I told Bud what I'd planned about looking for the missing cattle.

"Don't you want to go hunting?"

"I don't really care one way or the other," I answered. I'd been hunting a lot with my dad and always had fun and enjoyed it, until we got our deer or elk. That's when the work started.

"You better take a day and get a license. Take Sally with you, she can do some shopping and maybe you kids can take in an early movie. We've been so busy, we haven't had a chance to let you do what the other kids your age are doin'. I think that would be a good plan."

"If you say so," I answered.

"Plan on it and plan on getting your deer and elk. We pretty much live during the winter on wild meat," said Bud. "You don't think we'd eat our own beef, do you?"

Bud laughed at his own joke and I couldn't help but laugh also.

"You can go to town tomorrow. I'll tell Sally and she'll be ready."

"Where is she?" I hadn't seen her since supper.

"She's kinda tired," said Bud. "She went to bed early. I think it's her time of the month."

Bud didn't have to say anything else, I already knew what was going on. We'd had a very busy week, a lot of hard riding, and a lot of groundwork at the calving sheds. I could understand how Sally might be a little tired, but it was unlike her to not say goodnight to me. I wondered if she was sick.

The next morning Sally came to breakfast and looked all right. She was ready to go to town. We talked some on the way to town, and she fell asleep with her head on my shoulder. I wondered again if she was sick.

She woke up by the time we got to town.

"What are your plans?"

I guess I've got to get a huntin' license," I replied. "What do you want to do?"

"I'll do some shopping," she said. "Then we can take in a movie. We can see anything we want to."

I got my license, but only a deer tag. I needed to put in for a drawing to get an elk tag. I took Sally shopping and she got what she wanted, then we started looking for a movie house. We found a movie that Sally wanted to see and went in.

I lasted about fifteen or twenty minutes in the movie house before I fell asleep. Sally watched the whole show.

I wondered if I was sick, having fallen asleep like I did. I wasn't used to taking a nap. But I was kinda tired. We started home for the ranch.

"What did you think of the movie?"

"I don't know," I said. "I fell asleep. However, I enjoyed the cartoon."

"I noticed you fell asleep. Are you sick?"

"I'm kinda tired," I said. "How are you feelin'?"

"I'm okay," answered Sally. "I've been a little tired, but feel fine now."

We got home, unloaded Sally's purchases and I went to bed. I was tired. I slept good and woke up the next morning feeling fine. At breakfast, Sally indicated that she felt fine, however, Missus Abercrombie was feeling a little tired.

"I think there's a flu bug going around," said Pat, who was also feeling a little tired.

"Everybody take a little time off," said Bud. "I'm feeling a little tired also, everybody just relax today. I thought this feeling was just a let down after the busy part of the season, but there's definitely something happening. Just get the daily chores done and relax. Hunters are going to be arriving next week! We need everybody healthy."

For a week, we just did the daily chores and spent time relaxing. The following Thursday, hunters started showing up. Bud and Sally greeted them; Pat and I unloaded their gear and put it away in their assigned cabins.

Bud went over his hunting rules with each group of hunters at supper. He'd listed his hunting camp rules in the brochure he'd sent out when he received their deposits.

He explained to the hunters, "No drinking on the premises," said Bud. "Booze and loaded hunting rifles don't mix. Also, no loaded rifles in the cabins. All guns must be unloaded before putting them in the cabins. Also, don't shoot from horseback. If you see something you want to shoot at, get off your horse, tie him up or have someone hold him while you shoot. Any violation of these rules will result in your being told, not asked, to leave. If you're told to leave, you'll forfeit your deposit. And there is only one animal per tag. We're not going to let you take more than you're allotted. My brother, Fred, is the game warden out here, and he's just itching to bag someone on this ranch for a hunting violation. So make sure of your target. Any questions?"

The rules were simple.

I'd forgot about Bud's brother being the game warden and his other brother, Rod, and I poaching a deer some years ago, and feeding Fred a venison supper the very day we poached the deer. I smiled as I recalled the incident.

Opening morning of the season found us getting the hunters horseback early. The horses had been kept in overnight so we could get an early start. By sunrise, we had the hunters spaced out on ridges where we thought they might get a shot at a passing deer or elk. And we had their horses and the pack horses securely tied behind them. Pat, Sally, and I were riding below the hunters, seeing if we could scare up some game for them to shoot. Most of them had either-sex tags for deer, only a few had bull tags for elk.

Our ride below the hunters was successful. Some of the

hunters got shots at some buck deer. I rode up to find out if they were successful.

One hunter was successful. He'd killed a nice four-point buck and was field dressing it when I showed up. He was quite proud of his kill and kept referring to it as an "eight point."

"That's a four-point buck," I said. "You're usin' the eastern count. Out West here, we only count the points on one side."

"Well," said the hunter, "he's going back East, so he's an eight pointer!"

"Do you need some help cleaning that buck?"

"No," said the hunter.

"Anybody else get anything?"

"I think one of the other hunters got something, over that little rise," said the hunter.

"You wait here until I can find out what's happening," I said. "I'll bring your horse back when I come for you. Don't leave, we don't want to spend all day looking for a lost hunter."

The hunter smiled and went back to field dressing his deer. I set out to find the other hunter.

Pat had already found the hunter and was working in circles trying to find some tracks or blood of a wounded animal.

"I know I hit him," the hunter was saying. "I saw him jump and kick before he ran off!"

"Just stay there until I cut a track," said Pat. "I don't want you messin' up any sign."

Pat saw me ride up. "Come over here and help me try to find some sign, Honey!"

I rode over and began to look for any sign, be it blood or tracks. Soon I found a track.

"Here! There's tracks over here."

"Just hold still," said Pat, coming over to where I'd spotted the track.

"There's some blood on the grass over there," I said, pointing to where I'd spotted some blood.

"He did hit him," said Pat.

Pat must have doubted the hunter's claim that he hit the deer. A little farther on, there was more blood.

"He might be hit pretty good," said Pat, surveying the blood. "We'll wait here for a spell, and then track him. He might not be feeling so good an' will probably lay down."

We waited for a while and presently Sally showed up with the hunter I had found cleaning his deer. She had got his horse and he was horseback.

The hunter who had wounded the deer was becoming anxious and wanted to go find his deer. Pat convinced him to wait a little longer. "You don't want to drive the deer farther away, do you?"

After about fifteen minutes of waiting, Pat started to track the wounded animal. "You trail behind me about ten yards or so. Then, if I lose the trail, I'll be able to pick it up again. Honey, you lead his horse, and Sally, you lead mine. We'll find him sooner or later."

Pat tracked the animal for about a quarter of a mile, then suddenly stopped. He waved for the hunter to come forward and pointed ahead of them. In the brush, I could see a buck struggling to get up. He was weakened and in obvious pain.

The hunter went forward a few yards, raised his gun and fired. The buck dropped. He was out of pain.

We went forward to the dead deer and Pat immediately started to field dress him.

As he worked, Pat said, "Honey, you an' Sally ride back an' get the pack horses. Honey, you take that hunter an' get his deer loaded. Sally, you bring the other pack horse here an' we'll get this buck loaded. We can all start back toward the ranch when the deer are loaded. Honey, we'll catch up to you on the way."

Sally, the other hunter, and I started back to where the pack horses were tied and followed the instructions Pat had given us. We picked up some other hunters that weren't successful in the morning's hunt.

Pat soon caught up to us and we rode to the ranch. It was just about time for the noon meal, and I hadn't realized how hungry I was. Pat reminded everyone to unload their guns.

Sally was strangely quiet while we were eating. After we ate, the hunters went to their cabins. Sally and I sat out on the porch of the lodge.

She asked, "What did you think of this morning's hunt?"

"I suppose it was successful to some degree. Two of the hunters filled their tags."

"Yes, but did you see how that one deer suffered? And how hard he struggled to get up?"

"Yes," I answered. "But he didn't really suffer long. And the end came quickly when we got to him."

"I know," said Sally. "But somehow it seems sorta tragic."

"I think its better than starving to death during the winter," I said.

"I suppose you're right," answered Sally.

I found Bud and said, "We didn't feed this morning with the rush and excitement of getting the hunters out. I'll go take care of that now."

"Don't bother," said Bud. "I took care of that after you left. You go and relax a little before we take the hunters out this afternoon."

In the afternoon, we took the hunters out in the truck and placed them on ridges that hadn't been hunted. There were eight hunters that still had tags to fill.

One of the hunters filled his elk tag and I was glad we had the truck. It made getting the carcass back to the ranch easier. Two more hunters got their deer.

That night, Bud got instructions on how the hunters that had filled their tags wanted their meat cut.

"I'll take them to the meat cutters tomorrow and they'll be ready to go home with you when you leave. He'll have them packed on dry ice so they'll keep.

The next day went pretty much like the previous one. Up early, sitting on ridges looking for game. Pat and I had loaded the deer and elk carcasses onto the truck the night before and Bud would take them to town after he fed.

Most of the hunters that filled their tags stayed at the ranch, but some came with us. Their idea seemed to be, "We can help you ride the draws and such, resulting in a more successful drive."

We allowed them to come and Pat reminded them, "Keep your eyes open for cows. We're still missin' four pairs!"

The hunters thought he was referring to cow elk, but he quickly corrected them, "I mean beef cows!"

The hunt went well, with another couple of elk being taken and the remaining hunters filled their deer tags.

We went back to the ranch, unloaded the deer and elk we had packed, then Pat, Sally, and I went back for the deer and elk we couldn't pack. Both Pat and Bud were very adamant about not packing more than one hundred fifty pounds or so on any animal. We exceeded the limit slightly, but got everything back to the ranch in two trips.

We arrived back at the ranch shortly after Bud got back from town. The sun had gone down and it was beginning to get dark. Bud was on the porch having a discussion with the cook. Pat, Sally, and I had unpacked the pack horses, unsaddled them, and were unsaddling our own horses when Bud came into the barn, looking very upset.

"Put your gear away and come with me. Sally, you go to the lodge."

"I wonder what's up," I said.

"I got an idea," said Pat, "an' it ain't good."

Before we left the barn, Pat took his bullwhip down and carried it as we followed Bud to one of the cabins.

Bud knocked on the door, very politely.

From inside came a gravely voice, somewhat slurred, "Yeah, what da you want?"

Bud opened the door as one of the other fellas was reaching to open it from the inside.

"What's been going on here?"

I could tell from Bud's tone of voice that he wasn't happy. Apparently, this wasn't a social call.

"Our hunt is done," said one of the hunters. His speech was slurred. "We thought we'd just take it easy an' have a few drinks before dinner."

"A few drinks! You're drunk!" Bud picked up an almost empty bottle of bourbon off the table. "Take this and your other stuff and get off my ranch!"

The intoxicated hunter tried to get up, but lost his balance and fell to one knee. As he tried to get up, Pat pushed me aside, and said, "Give me some room, Honey. This might develop into something!"

The drunken hunter got up, grabbed a chair and started toward Bud. Pat unleashed the bull whip and it snaked across the room, wrapping itself around one of the legs of the chair. Pat gave a good hard pull on the whip, and the chair and hunter hit the floor.

One of the hunters that had been with us during the day went to the hunter on the floor, saying, "I'm sorry, Mister Wilson. I never knew he even had anything to drink with him. I went over all the rules with these guys before we left home. I'm really sorry!"

"Well," said Bud, "like he said, his hunt is over. You take him and all your stuff and your whole party and get off my ranch!

You got fifteen minutes. The cook has already called the sheriff and he's probably on his way, along with the game warden."

Pat went and loosened his bullwhip from the chair. The sober hunter was helping the drunk to his feet.

"Wha ... what happened?" The drunk was a little bewildered.

"We're leaving," replied the sober hunter. "All because of you!"

The other hunters in the room had started to pack their things.

"How come?"

"Because you're drunk!" The sober hunter was obviously upset with him and beginning to lose his temper.

Bud brought out some papers, looked through them and gave some of them to the sober hunter. "These are your claim tickets for your meat. You decide what to do with them. Just to make sure nothing leaves here that isn't supposed to go, we'll watch you load up. Better get going now, you've only got fourteen minutes left. You've also forfeited your deposit—there's no refund."

As the hunters started to load their gear, Bud took the sober hunter aside and told him, "You better drive them into town. The sheriff's headed out here and he'd like nothing more than arrest some hunters for drunk driving. I'm not sure any of them are capable of driving safely. If you leave anything here, I'll mail it to you. We're going to have to do a complete house cleaning here and air the cabin out completely. Better get a move on, you're running short of time."

Once again the sober hunter apologized to Bud.

Bud accepted his apology with a nod of his head, but didn't say anything.

The other hunters were loading their stuff, grumbling and getting more upset with the drunk. They weren't a very happy bunch.

The drunken hunter was trying to get his stuff loaded and

while he was taking his rifle out, he stumbled and the gun went off.

"That does it! That's the last straw! A loaded gun in one of my cabins! GET OFF MY PROPERTY, RIGHT NOW!" Bud was clearly angry. I'd never seen him like this before.

Before the hunters could leave, a car with red lights flashing on the roof pulled into the yard.

It was the game warden. He got out of the car and came to the cabin. There wasn't an acknowledgement between Bud and his brother, the game warden.

"I heard a shot and this late at night, I thought someone might be spotlighting some deer," said the game warden. "I thought I ought to get here as fast as I could."

"Glad you came, Fred. We're inviting these folks to leave. There's a few of them drunk and one of them had a loaded rifle in the cabin. He stumbled and the gun fired. That was the shot you heard. I don't think anybody got hit, but there's a hole in the floor. You know my rules, and they've busted the two most important. So they're gone."

The sight of the badge on the game warden tended to sober up the hunters some. An official badge on a uniform can have a very sobering effect.

"The sheriff is coming. He said on the radio he was about five minutes behind me. Do you want to hold these guys until he gets here?"

"I don't know, what do you think? What could we hold them on?" Bud was weighing out his options.

"Drunk and disorderly is one charge. Firing a gun inside a dwelling is a certain indication they're not orderly. It's not up to me," said Fred. "It's your decision completely."

The hunters were listening to the conversation as they loaded their stuff. Fearing possible legal difficulties if they stayed around any longer, one of them said, "I think we're ready to go."

As he said that, another car pulled up. It was the sheriff. "What's going on here? I heard there were some problems that I might need to check out."

"I think it's all under control, officer," said the sober hunter. "We're just getting ready to leave. Give me the keys, Richard, I'll drive."

"That's my car! I'll do the driving!" The drunken hunter got in the car and started the engine.

"You can get him on drunken driving charges right now, sheriff," said Fred. "He's behind the wheel and the car is running."

"You can also get him on assault charges." The cook had come down from the lodge. He had a black eye. "He punched me when I wouldn't give him some pop to use as mixer for his bourbon. I'll be glad to press charges."

The sheriff stepped over to the car. "Get out of the car, sir. It's apparent that you have been drinking and you're behind the wheel of a running motor vehicle. Also, this man says you punched him. I'm placing you under arrest for drunk driving and assault."

The drunken hunter started to get out of the car and fell to the ground, face first. While he was down, the sheriff held him down with one knee and handcuffed him. He then helped him up and placed him in the back of his car.

"Your cook will need to come to town and fill out some papers tomorrow," said the sheriff. "I can only hold him for twenty-four hours on the drunken driving charge."

"You boys better follow them to town. I just want you off my ranch. And when you get gone don't even think of coming back! Ever!"

The hunters got in the car. The sober hunter drove off, but not before he apologized to Bud again.

Bud's only comment was, "Just be gone!"

Pat started for the lodge. "I think the excitement's over an' I'm hungry. What are you burnin' for us for supper, Cookie?"

"It's ready an' it ain't burnt," said the cook.

As we went to the lodge, Bud said, "You didn't tell me he'd hit you and I didn't notice the black eye. How are you feeling? Fred, you better come and eat with us."

"I'm okay," replied the cook. "But I'd better hurry to the kitchen. I might be burning something!"

Conversation at supper that night was lively, mostly talking about the previous events of the evening. After supper, Sally and I sat on the porch.

She asked, "What did you do during the affair of the evening?"

"Nothing," I said. "When the drunk started toward your dad with the chair, I started toward him. But Pat pushed me aside an' pulled him down with the whip. I did get close to your dad, just in case one of the other fellers decided to try something, an' I kept an eye on 'em. There wasn't much to it. I've never seen your dad like that, I was a little surprised."

"This is Dad's ranch and he makes the rules. With regard to the hunters, he's really strict, and won't allow any infraction of his rules."

"How come?"

Sally got real serious. "My mother was killed by a hunter cleaning his supposedly empty rifle. I was only about two and don't remember it. That's why Daddy is so strict with the hunters."

"Why does he take 'em? He certainly doesn't have to."

"But he does," replied Sally. "The ranch has had some pretty tough years in the past and we're just starting to come out of it. One of the reasons Dad is trying to pay more attention to the cattle aspect of this ranch is to make it more profitable. That's why Dad has invested in his little feedlot, got the replacement heifers artificially bred, and went into the paint horse business.

When we get a little farther ahead, Daddy will stop taking the hunters. I understand, in the past, he's actually had to borrow some money from Missus Abercrombie just to keep the place afloat. I don't know how much, but he's getting her paid off, slowly but surely. And he's spent a lot of money sending me back East to that fancy boarding school."

"I wasn't aware of all that," I said. "There's a lot going on here that I'm not familiar with."

"You know all you need to know to take care of our cattle and horses and you've really made great improvements with the dudes."

I wasn't aware of any great improvements I'd made with the dudes. I generally kept my mouth shut and spoke only when I was asked a question, or could offer some advice to our wannabe cowboys. I didn't engage much in any idle conversation. Of course, I did react to the humorous things the dudes said and did.

The next day, Bud and the cook went to town to take care of the legalities with the hunters. They returned late in the afternoon and said that the offending hunter had gotten out of jail on bail, and would have to return in a couple of months for trial. Bud and the cook would have to go to town for trial, but it would be during a slower time of year.

We had another bunch of hunters come in the following week and were fairly successful in helping them get their game.

After the hunting season was over, Bud said, "I'll be glad when we don't have to take in hunters. Even though the money's good, it's a problem. It does create a lot of extra work. Now we can spend our time taking care of the ranch."

Missus Abercrombie announced at supper one night that she was going to spend the winter at the ranch by saying, "As long as this young lady is staying here this winter, I intend to stay also. I couldn't leave with a clear conscience knowing she'd be here alone with you three ruffians!"

"That's all right, Virginia. You can help when needed," said Bud.

One day, Bud got a call from a neighboring ranch. After the call was over, Bud came to me and said, "Our missing cows and calves have been found. They're at the neighbor's ranch. They're holding them in the corral at the main ranch and we can pick them up tomorrow. Honey, I want you to take my two-ton truck and go get them. I'll draw you a map so you can get there easily. Bring them home and turn them loose with the older cows. Separate the calves, we might fatten them up and use them to feed the dudes next summer."

Sally said, "I'd like to go with you. There's not much to do around here now. The ride will do me some good."

After the feeding chores were done the next day, I got the ranch's two-ton truck, got a map from Bud on where to find the place, and Sally and I headed out. It was a nice drive and it did provide a change of scenery. I remarked about the change of scenery to Sally.

"Tomorrow, I'll take you for a ride and show you some scenery I don't think you've seen before," she said. "It's a very special area and it's very beautiful."

"You're on," I said. "But is this goin' to be a dude ride? Does that mean you're goin' to saddle my horse for me?"

Sally slapped my shoulder and laughed. "You're perfectly capable of saddling your own horse!"

We got to the neighbor's ranch. I recognized the foreman from meeting him on the range when I was going home last year. He showed us where the cows were and helped us load them. We thanked him and made ready to leave.

"If you come across any of our cows, give me a call. I'll come and get them. We're still missing a few."

"You bet I will," I said.

The ride home was uneventful. Sally did most of the talk-

ing and mostly about the upcoming wedding next spring. I con-
curred with everything she said she wanted; it was her deal. She
was keeping it fairly simple and I appreciated that.

We put the cows in a corral. We'd saddle some horses in the
morning and take the cows out to the cow herd after we fed. We
put the calves with the other calves and called it a day.

A Special Place

The following day, after we fed, we saddled a couple of horses and went for a ride. We started out on one of the regular trails and then took a seldom-used trail off to the north. This trail hadn't been used much and led to a secluded little valley about a mile behind the lodge. The entire valley was fenced off, prohibiting any cattle or horses from grazing it. The fenced area probably enclosed about ten acres total.

It was a pretty little valley, only about five or six acres of open space. It was surrounded by pines on the south and aspen trees on the north. Sally got to the gate and got off her horse to open the wire gate.

"This really is a dude ride," I said, as I rode through the gate that Sally held open. I tipped my hat to Sally and said, "I sure do appreciate that, Miss Sally. I think it's about time I got some of the respect I truly deserve!"

She laughed, got on her horse and we rode into the valley. I noticed how the grass hadn't been grazed all summer. In the middle of the valley was a wrought iron fence and there were headstones within the enclosure.

"This is the family graveyard," said Sally. "Dad's grandfather, grandmother, his father and mother are buried here. There are some other members of the family also buried here. There are also some long time ranch hands here. This is where my mother is buried and Dad says he wants to be buried here, too, right next to her."

We got off our horses and tied them to the fence. As we walked among the headstones, Sally told me about the various residents.

"You know," she said, "I really love this ranch. I don't really want to leave it. And I want to be buried right here when I die. And, if you wish, you can be buried right here also, right beside me."

I hadn't given any thought to dying. I was still young and thought I had my whole life ahead of me, but Sally had apparently given the subject some thought.

I asked, "What's all this thinkin' about dyin'?"

"I don't think about it all the time, silly," she said, as she laughed and slapped my shoulder. "But I am prepared. Daddy has brought me up here and told me the family history many times. Quite often, he'll come up here by himself and just do some thinking. To him, this is a very spiritual spot."

We left the family graveyard without me saying another word. I didn't know what to say.

Winter came and we settled into a winter routine. We had the replacement heifers in the feedlot to feed. The older cows were out on pasture. We'd turned the saddle horses out, keeping in only a few horses we needed during the winter. I kept the two year olds I'd started in for the winter, thinking I'd use them as much as I could. Sally kept her grulla colt and another horse. Pat kept two of his horses and Bud kept in his big paint.

We were pretty well set for the winter when the snow came and stayed.

Bud and the cook went to town for the trial of the drunken hunter. He was found guilty and sentenced to a few years in prison on the assault charge, but his sentence was suspended and he got a few years more on probation. The judge also issued a restraining order prohibiting him from ever entering the Wilson ranch again.

Before Bud went to town, Sally convinced him to see the doctor and have a checkup. She even made the appointment for Bud and made the cook promise that he'd make sure Bud kept the appointment.

Other Books by Stu Campbell

Horsing Around a Lot

Horsing Around the Dudes

Humor Around Horses

You Can't Be Serious!

Comedy Around the Corral

More Humor Around Horses

A Young Cowboy's Adventure

Honey